I HAVE AN IDEA

Jeremy D Scholz

This is a work of fiction. Names, characters, places, and events are either the product of the author's imagination or used fictitiously. Any resemblance to actual persons, living or dead, or actual events is purely coincidental.

For information or permission requests, contact:

Jeremy D Scholz

https://jeremydscholz.com/

ISBN: 979-8-9994313-0-1

Printed in the United States of America

First Edition

I Have an Idea

by Jeremy D Scholz

jeremydscholz.com

Cover design by: Getcovers.com

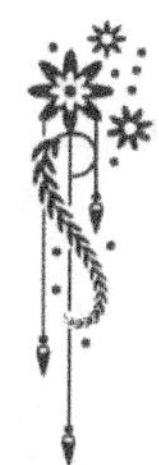

DEDICATION

I dedicated this book to my son, Merrick. He was the purpose of my life.

To many, he was overwhelming, too much energy to handle. He was endlessly curious, asking so many questions that most found it exhausting, perhaps because he pushed them to the limits of their understanding.

But, to those who gave him a place in their lives, he was the most spontaneous of friends: loyal, caring, and full of life.

He was my biggest fan in every new endeavor I pursued, and I was his; I cheered him on at every turn.

He would have loved this story. It breaks my heart that I couldn't finish it before he was taken from me. His voice echoes through these pages, and I miss his constant spark, his joyful cry: "I have an idea!"

CONTENTS

INTRODUCTION

Some stories begin with fireworks. Others whisper.

This one begins in an ordinary corner of a high school portable sequestered in the back of the school, an unexpected friendship, a sentence spoken without pomp, and the kind of idea that can turn a life upside down, or maybe the way it was supposed to be.

This is a story about moments, the ones we dread, the ones that catch us off guard, and the ones that allow us to catch our breath for a moment. About people who crash into our lives and change everything. About love, not the kind from movies, but the kind we resist, and it grows in cracked places of our lives and holds on tight.

I Have an Idea isn't just about two teenagers. It's about daring to believe in something more when the world gives you less. It's about fierce loyalty, impossible choices, and the fragile beauty of second chances.

If you've ever felt like your story wasn't good enough, or like you had nothing to offer, this book is for you. Because sometimes all it takes is one wild idea, and someone brave enough to say it out loud.

Let's begin,

J.S.

CHAPTER 1

Ethan Parker stood outside the school gates, staring at the buildings that had always blended into the backdrop of his everyday routine. This morning, though, they looked different—less like places of learning and more like looming monuments to his shame. Today was not typical. Not for Ethan.

He shifted the strap of his backpack and inhaled deeply, the familiar scent of morning dew on concrete oddly grounding. For the first time in his school career, he was in trouble. Real trouble. Not the *forgot-your-homework, serve-a-detention* kind of trouble, but in-school suspension kind of trouble.

One stupid moment. One bad choice. And now—three days. Three days of being grouped with the so-called *problem kids*.

I'm not one of them, Ethan told himself, trying to convince the part of his brain that wasn't already spiraling.

He hadn't even stepped on campus yet. Denial, maybe. Or fear. Or both. He didn't even know where the detention room was. It felt like being punished in a foreign country with no map.

Finally, he steadied himself, clenched his jaw, and pushed through the front doors to the office.

The secretary barely glanced up from her screen, typing furiously with acrylic nails that clacked like tiny hammers. She looked every bit as overwhelmed as he felt.

"I'm... supposed to be in detention?" Ethan said, his voice uncertain.

The secretary didn't bother hiding her annoyance. She snatched a pink slip from a stack and scribbled something on it. "Portable behind the arboretum."

Ethan blinked. "We have an arboretum?"

"Apparently," she muttered, already dismissing him with a wave.

As he walked away, Ethan let out a low chuckle. This day was already surreal. The further he walked into the back corners of campus, the more unfamiliar everything looked. How had he been here for three years and never noticed this whole area? Cracked pavement gave way to weedy patches of grass. The arboretum—if it could even be called that—was a small, fenced grove of trees, overgrown but strangely peaceful. And nestled behind it like a forgotten shed stood the portable.

He paused for a moment, then pulled the door open.

Inside, fluorescent lights buzzed overhead, and the smell of old books and cheap cologne hung in the air. The room was nearly empty. One adult sat behind a desk, hunched over a battered newspaper.

Ethan approached him slowly and handed over his pink slip.

The man, gray-bearded and heavy-eyed, grumbled, "Sit in a chair."

No seating chart? Ethan thought. *Is this lawless territory? Some kind of academic purgatory?*

He sat in the far corner of the room, near a dusty bookcase. His eyes scanned the titles—some classics, some trashy pulp novels, and a couple of dog-eared poetry collections. He exhaled. *Okay. Maybe I can survive this.*

One by one, students trickled in. Some looked amused, others indifferent. Two seats remained: one beside the teacher, one beside him.

Ethan braced himself. *Just don't be anyone I know. Please.*

The door burst open.

And there she was.

Janet.

The chaos of his middle school memories came flooding back like a nightmare wearing eyeliner. She looked the same—only taller, more dangerous somehow. Her hair was still that same deep brown, tangled and unbothered, and her smirk hadn't aged a day.

Ethan's heart sank. *Why her?* Out of all people.

She walked with that same unbothered swagger, straight toward him.

"Hey, I know you," she said, sliding into the seat beside him without hesitation.

Ethan stiffened. "I don't want to talk to you."

Janet leaned back in her chair, unfazed. "We went to middle school together, didn't we?"

Don't you remember what you did to me? he wanted to shout. *How you made me feel like a bug under a magnifying glass?*

"Go away," he said flatly.

Her smile widened. "Touchy. I'm not gonna bite."

Ethan's voice rose, sharper now. "Do you not remember how rude and insufferable you were back then?"

She looked at him like he was reciting trivia about someone else's life. "Who has time to dwell on the past?" she said, grinning like a sage who had just dropped a life-changing quote.

"Just leave me alone," he muttered, staring down at the desk.

But Janet was just getting started. She slowly dragged her desk an inch closer. Then another. Until they were side by side.

She rested her chin on her arms and just stared at him.

Ethan sighed. He tried not to look. He turned his head ever so slightly, catching a glimpse of her sideways. She was waiting for it.

"I knew you couldn't ignore me," she whispered.

Ethan sighed again. "Why—do you like tormenting me?"

Her laugh, loud and unashamed, pierced the room.

Mr. Bottoms glanced up over his paper, furrowed his brow. "Knock it off."

He quickly returned to the world of ink and print.

Janet gave Ethan a playful shove. "Come on, I'm just messing around. It helps with the boredom."

He resisted the urge to roll his eyes. *This is going to be the longest three days of my life.*

Ethan stared at the clock: 9:07 a.m.

Time had stopped. Or at least agreed to die a slow, agonizing death.

The room buzzed with fluorescent lights and the distant hum of lawnmowers somewhere outside the windowless portable. Ethan couldn't block it all out like he normally would.

Mr. Bottoms hadn't looked up from his newspaper in over twenty minutes.

Janet drummed her fingers on her desk. Loudly.

Tap-tap-tap. Tap-tap-tap.

Ethan clenched his jaw. *Don't engage. She's like a raccoon, ignore her and maybe she'll move on.*

"You still mad at me?" Janet asked, her voice far too cheerful for the setting.

Ethan didn't look up. "No. I'm mad at the clock."

Janet grinned. "Oooh, sarcasm. So, you do speak."

He sighed and flipped a page in his book. "I'm trying to pass the time, not add to my sentence."

"Well, forgive me for attempting to make this hellhole entertaining," Janet protested.

"You could try being quiet," he muttered.

"Where's the fun in that?" she shot back, then leaned over, lowering her voice. "You're not still salty about middle school, are you?"

Ethan lowered the book slowly. "You called me 'Neck Zit' for three months straight."

Janet burst out laughing. "That was you?! I thought that was Jason White."

He didn't laugh. "It wasn't."

"Oh." She blinked, realizing she had hurt him. "Okay. Yeah, that was messed up. I was kind of a menace back then."

"You *were* a menace," he agreed.

Janet tilted her head, pretending to be touched. "Aw, you remember."

Ethan rolled his eyes and picked up the book again.

A few minutes of silence passed. She started humming. Loudly. Off-key.

"Seriously?" he snapped.

"You didn't say there was a rule against music," Janet contended.

"Pretty sure Mr. Bottoms would, if he could hear anything over that sports section," Ethan huffed.

Janet snorted. "He's counting time, just like you, apparently."

Ethan tried to go back to reading, but the words on the page were just a blur. Janet had a gravitational pull—chaotic, loud, and impossible to tune out.

"So, what's your deal now?" she asked. "Still in the honors program? Still writing stories in your notebook?"

He glanced at her. "Still judging people for fun?"

"Only the ones who take themselves too seriously," she said with a smirk.

Ethan smirked despite himself. "Then you must love me."

"Love's a strong word," she replied. "But you're definitely growing on me."

"I'm not a fungus," he objected.

She gave a sly smile. "Could've fooled me."

Another pause.

"Do you remember anything nice about middle school?" Ethan asked suddenly.

Janet leaned back and stared at the ceiling. "Hmmm… I liked lunch."

"That's not a memory—that's survival," Ethan challenged.

"Okay, fine." She looked at him. "I remember dodgeball. I was good at nailing people in the face."

"Yeah. I remember," he said somberly.

"Oh no, did I hit you?" Janet asked.

Ethan subconsciously rubbed his nose where the ball had hit him. "Twice."

"You're tough—no way a ball hurt you," she said.

"No. I had braces," he confessed.

"Yikes." Janet cringed.

He nodded. "I bled onto my shirt, and you laughed."

Janet winced, finally understanding she had actually hurt him. "Okay, okay—I suck. That's fair."

"I'm glad you agree." He appreciated her owning it.

She grinned. "So, are we bonding or fighting?"

"I think it's more like… coexisting under duress."

"I'll take it," Janet noted.

More silence. The clock ticked to 9:41.

Janet kicked his foot under the table.

Ethan looked up. "What?"

"Just checking to make sure you're not frozen in time," she said matter-of-factly.

He narrowed his eyes. "Do you ever stop talking?"

Janet shrugged. "Only when I'm asleep or unconscious."

"I can work with that," Ethan said with a smirk.

She chuckled, folding her arms behind her head. "This is going to be fun."

Ethan went back to his book. He didn't answer, but something told him she might be right.

CHAPTER 2

The next morning, Ethan walked the campus like a ghost. Detached. Unseen.

But there was something liberating in that. For once, he wasn't rushing to class or buried in his phone. He was looking.

He noticed initials carved into a tree: J.A. + K.S. Probably long-forgotten lovebirds.

He lingered by the flower beds. Had they always been there?

He paused at the chirping of birds, picking out the differences in their calls. A family of squirrels darted across his path, the young ones chasing each other.

This place is alive, he thought. *How did I never see any of it?*

The bell startled him. He sprinted to the portable.

Inside, his old seat was open. But Janet's was taken by another kid—headphones in, already zoned out. Ethan grinned. Maybe the universe was giving him a break.

He reached for a book, but before he could crack the spine—

SLAM. The door flew open.

Janet entered like she owned the place. Leather jacket. Combat boots. Hair in a messy bun that somehow looked artfully styled.

"Great," she muttered. "Another day in paradise."

Ethan stifled a laugh, coughing to hide it. He glanced at Mr. Bottoms, who was deeply engaged in sorting papers like it was a life-or-death mission. Ethan couldn't believe how little the man seemed to care.

Then came Janet's voice.

"Get out of my seat, punk."

The boy looked at Ethan, who gave a helpless shrug. The boy groaned and moved.

Janet dropped her desk right beside Ethan again, like a magnet locking into place.

Strangely, Ethan didn't feel annoyed. He felt… curious.

"What are you looking at, brainiac?" Janet asked, smirking as she caught him sneaking a glance.

"Nothing," he mumbled. "Just… I think your jacket is kinda cool."

"Flattery will get you nowhere," she said—but Ethan caught the slight twitch of her lips, like she wasn't used to compliments and didn't know how to wear one.

Janet tossed her jacket on the back of her chair, then slumped into it like royalty bored with her kingdom.

"Did ya miss me, Parker?" she asked, stretching her legs until her boot tapped the leg of his desk.

Ethan looked at her suspiciously.

"I didn't tell you my last name. How…"

With a grin that was adorable and menacing at the same time, she pointed to his backpack, where his name was written in black marker.

"So, you *did* miss me?"

"No," Ethan replied without looking up. "But I missed the existential dread, so… close enough."

Janet grinned. "You're getting funnier. I think I'm rubbing off on you."

Ethan glanced at her. "Is that what you tell your probation officer?"

"Only if I want her to roll her eyes at me," she said, mock-proud.

They lapsed into silence for a bit. Ethan read. Janet doodled in the margins of her notebook, chewing her pen cap. After a while, she noticed Ethan staring blankly at a page.

"Okay, either that book is written in ancient Greek or you're thinking too hard."

He looked at her. Then back down. Then up again.

"I just… I think I blend into the background too much. Most days, it's like no one notices I'm there unless I mess up."

Janet blinked, caught off guard.

"Whoa. Mood shift. You, okay?"

"I'm not looking for sympathy," Ethan muttered.

"That's good, because I suck at it," Janet said—but her voice softened.

"Why do you feel invisible?"

He nodded slowly.

"Like I'm the guy people forget was at the party, or the kid teachers remember as 'the quiet one.' It's weird. You spend years trying to be good, to stay out of trouble, and all it gets you is… forgotten."

Janet tapped her pen against her notebook, thoughtful.

"You're not forgettable."

"You remembered the zit nickname. Not me."

"Okay, fair," she said with a sheepish smirk. "But still. You're… different now. You push back. I notice that."

He blinked.

"That almost sounded like a compliment."

"Don't let it go to your head." She hesitated.

"Want to hear something weird? I wrote a poem about stuff like that. Sort of."

Ethan raised an eyebrow.

"You write poetry?"

"Wait—seriously?" Ethan said, surprised.

She shrugged.

"Sometimes. Helps me not punch walls."

She flipped through her notebook and tore out a page, its edges jagged. After a moment, she read it aloud:

"Fire Breather"

There's a girl in the mirror with a cinder on her tongue,

Saying things, she doesn't mean but can't be undone.

She smiles like a matchbook,

But inside she's low.

Breaking the silence to cage her mind,

Wanting peace but finding it slow.

She hides all her bruises beneath paper and ink,

Pretends she's in control but starting to sink.

Don't ask her to be quiet,

She can't be kept still.

She's lit the fuse.

What happens next will reveal.

She folded the paper back up, not meeting his eyes.

Ethan didn't speak right away; he hadn't expected vulnerability.

"…That's really good," he said at last, almost surprised. "It's raw. It's kind of… sad."

Janet shrugged.

"Anger's easier to carry than fear. And I got a lot of both."

He nodded.

"You ever shown anyone your stuff?"

She gave a dry laugh.

"Nope. You're the first. Congratulations—you're now my unpaid therapist."

Ethan smirked.

"I'll send you the bill later."

They sat in silence again, but this time, it was comfortable. The edge between them hadn't vanished, but it had defiantly softened.

"So," Janet said, twirling her pen, "you're invisible, and I'm a walking fire hazard. We make a weird pair."

"Yeah," Ethan said, flipping a page in his book, "but at least the company's not boring."

Janet grinned sideways at him.

"Careful, Parker. Keep talking like that and I might start thinking you like me."

He gave her a dry look.

"Let's not get carried away."

But the corner of his mouth twitched—just slightly.

Janet saw it.

It was quiet again for a while.

She crossed her arms.

"So, what did you do to end up in the Hall of Shame?"

Ethan hesitated, then exhaled.

"I threw a kid's backpack across the room. The teacher, Mrs. Thompson, saw me do it—but she didn't hear what the kid said to upset me."

Janet gave a low whistle.

"That's always the way. They catch the reaction, never the action."

"He said something about my dad." Ethan looked down at his desk.

"Good for you—" She paused. "Gee, thanks."

"No, I mean… for sticking up for your family," Janet said, sounding sincere.

"Detention isn't so bad. It's kind of a badge of honor."

Ethan raised an eyebrow.

"A badge of honor? Is that what you tell yourself every time you get thrown in here?"

She shrugged.

"Better than being another obedient little cog in the school machine."

Ethan considered her response.

"Why do you get into so many fights?" Ethan asked. He had told her why he was there; it was only fair to ask.

"I didn't get in a fight this time. In class, a kid was rude, so I told him off. When the teacher called me out, she

wouldn't let me explain, so I told her to go screw herself." Janet shrugged.

"I would've just taken it. Good for you for defending yourself," Ethan said honestly.

"I can't back down from a fight. It's a problem," Janet admitted.

"I have anger issues. I don't know. I just can't back down." She shrugged again.

Ethan thought about it, then asked,

"Do you like to fight?"

"You're bringing me down. I may have to fight you," Janet said without much conviction.

Then, without warning, she wrapped her arms around Ethan's arm and rested her head on his shoulder. Ethan didn't pull away. She had opened up to him, and he respected that.

Janet let go abruptly.

"I didn't mean to do that."

This day passed much quicker than the last, and Ethan felt like he understood Janet a little better.

Maybe there was more to this insane, hot-headed bully.

He never thought he'd find comfort in a punishment—or in a person he never wanted to see.

But he was.

Surviving.

Maybe even changing.

CHAPTER 3

By the third day, Ethan felt like a seasoned detention convict. He knew where to go and understood the routine. He still wasn't completely comfortable, but it didn't feel as much like punishment anymore. He didn't even dread seeing Janet—she really wasn't the menace he remembered. People can change.

The engine grumbled as it slowed to a stop in Ethan's favorite spot, a gravel-throated growl that echoed across the nearly empty student parking lot. Ethan shifted the 1975 Camaro into park, the stick catching like always. He sighed and gave the cracked steering wheel a pat.

"Still alive," he murmured. "Barely."

The Camaro had once been a dream in faded cherry red. It was his father's dream to restore a car like the one he drove as a teenager. He'd only gotten as far as the engine

before cancer stole the rest of the build from him. Now, Ethan saw it as his mission to keep the car running—patch by patch, paycheck by paycheck. The body was dull, the upholstery cracked, but it moved. And that was enough. He remembered his dad every time he drove it.

Ethan stepped out, tugging the strap of his backpack over his shoulder.

"Surprise, nerd!" A body slammed into his back—not hard enough to hurt, but enough to make him stagger. Thin arms looped around his shoulders like an ambush vine.

"What the—Janet?!" He instinctively caught her legs as they wrapped around his waist. She was laughing like a maniac, her boots thudding against his thighs. "Why are you on me?"

"It's early. I'm tired. You're big. I'm small. It made sense to me," Janet explained.

Ethan groaned. "You can't just jump on people. That's illegal in most states."

Janet rested her chin on his shoulder. "What are you gonna do, drop me?"

"I should," he mumbled.

"But you won't," she said smugly. "Because deep down, you're just a big ol' softie who'd feel bad if he let a little girl crack her head on the pavement."

Ethan rolled his eyes—but he didn't let her go. "You're insufferable."

"And you're surprisingly comfortable." Janet gave him a squeeze.

He started walking. Her weight was surprisingly manageable. Years of hauling lumber and tools for his uncle made this feel more like an inconvenience than a challenge.

As they moved across the parking lot, Ethan said, "You know, if anyone sees this, they're gonna think we're, you know, like a thing."

Janet gasped dramatically. "A *thing*? You mean people will start writing our names in cute little hearts in their notebooks? We'd better get a cool ship name. *Janthan? Ethn-et?* Wait—*Jankins?*"

"Ew. Stop." His resistance was meager.

"Never," she said affectionately.

Ethan passed a cluster of underclassmen who blinked in disbelief as she made a shocking hand gesture their way—in a very Janet manner.

"Why are you doing this?" he asked finally.

She shrugged. "Because it's weird. And fun. And you looked kinda down, so I jumped on you."

"I don't always think about the why," she admitted.

They reached the back of campus, the arboretum and its sleepy trees still dripping with dew. The portable loomed ahead—still ugly. Still cold.

"I can walk the rest of the way," Janet said, sliding off his back like she hadn't just turned his spine into a jungle gym. "Now that I know you give rides, I'll be expecting them. I think of you as my emotional support mule."

Ethan adjusted his backpack and gave her a side glance. "You're exhausting."

Janet grinned. "You're welcome."

"I have an idea," she said.

Ethan muttered, "Oh no."

"This one is tame. We should explore the tree place. We've got time—the bell doesn't ring for another ten minutes," she added, grabbing his hand and pulling him toward the path.

Ethan didn't fight it. He'd already learned it was pointless to talk her out of an idea. Besides, it was a decent one. He was curious about the arboretum.

He pointed out the initials carved into one of the trees.

Janet traced them with her finger, smiling thoughtfully. "I wonder where they are now?"

Ethan noticed the color of her hair in the sunlight. *It wasn't just brown—there were layers of gold, copper, maybe even a hint of auburn. It was... pretty.*

He quickly shook his head, snapping himself out of the thought before she noticed him looking.

"It's interesting, right? It's evidence that they were here. So many people come and go, and there's no trace of them," Ethan said.

"Like they weren't seen," Janet replied—not as a jab, but as a connection to the sentiment.

The bell rang, and they headed toward their last day of detention.

As they approached the door, she said quietly, "That car of yours sounds angry."

Ethan paused. "It was my dad's. He was rebuilding it before he got sick."

Janet nodded, her face unexpectedly serious. "So, you keep it running for him?"

"Yeah," Ethan said, voice soft.

"That's… beautiful," she said, surprising even herself. "Ugly car. Beautiful reason."

Ethan chuckled. "You really don't know when to stop talking, do you?"

"Nope. Not even a little," she confirmed.

Without meaning to, they walked into their third day of detention together—like two people who maybe weren't enemies anymore. Not quite friends, but not alone either.

Their seats were taken by two new detention students.

"I got this!" Janet proclaimed. "Move it, squids—those are our seats."

Ethan had to admire Janet's willingness to stick up for herself. He wanted the same seat, but he would've just taken another.

The boys looked to Mr. Bottoms for help but quickly realized they were on their own. They moved to other seats, and Ethan and Janet reclaimed their usual spot. Janet immediately dragged her desk right next to his.

Ethan looked at her, changing tactics. She looked back—but he held the eye contact.

"What?" she snapped.

Ethan grinned, enjoying this new dynamic. He opened his book, pleased with himself for getting a reaction out of her.

"Hey, if you're going to sit there and read, why don't you read to me?" Janet asked.

Ethan studied her face. There was no malice in her eyes.

"Okay. If you want me to."

Janet listened intently. Ethan's voice was soothing, and the day passed faster than they realized.

As the clock ticked toward the end of detention, Janet stood, her confidence radiating through the room.

"Don't think this is the last you'll see of me, Ethan," she said with a grin. "Next time, you're coming with me for some real fun."

Ethan grinned back. The thought was a little intimidating. "We'll see about that."

Janet walked alongside Ethan. The late afternoon sun painted long golden shadows across the asphalt. The parking lot had mostly emptied, and the old Camaro stood out like a relic from another time—faded, dented in places, but holding itself together with quiet pride.

Janet leaned casually against the passenger-side door, her leather jacket creaking softly as she tilted her head toward him.

"Would you want to drop me off at my place?" she asked. Her voice was surprisingly respectful, almost soft.

Ethan raised an eyebrow. He'd expected some kind of dramatic flair or a smart remark—not this. Her hesitation caught him off guard; she wasn't the type to hesitate.

He knew arguing would be a waste of energy.

"Fine," he sighed, unlocking the door with a mechanical click. "But you're giving me the location of your secret lair. You sure you want to do that?"

Janet grinned. "You seem trustworthy enough, Camaro Boy."

As she climbed in, Ethan felt a strange tension. Not the kind born of resentment, but something subtler— curiosity tangled with caution. She was the only person who'd been in the car since his dad died.

The moment they pulled out of the lot, Janet started poking around like a raccoon with opposable thumbs. She twisted the air vent toward her face, pressed a few buttons on the crusty old radio, and flicked a small switch under the dash.

"What does this one do?" she asked, already flicking it.

Ethan winced. "It used to turn on the dome light."

A faint click sounded, followed by silence. The dome light stayed off.

Another piece of his connection to his dad broke.

Janet turned to him slowly, guilt washing over her expression like a tide. "Oh my God. I didn't mean to break something."

Ethan took a slow breath, his jaw tightening. "It's fine. Just... please don't touch anything else."

Janet's teasing demeanor vanished. She sat back, folding her hands in her lap.

"I'm sorry," she said, eyes dropping. "I didn't know. I wasn't trying to be a jerk."

Ethan glanced at her, then returned his focus to the road. "Yeah, I know. You're just Janet."

She smiled faintly at that. For the next few minutes, the ride was quiet, filled only by the rumble of the engine

and the occasional squeak of the suspension. Janet glanced at him out of the corner of her eye, unsure if she should speak again.

"Thank you for the ride," she said eventually, softer than before. "And for not kicking me out when I acted like a gremlin."

Ethan sighed, a corner of his mouth twitching upward. "Just don't break anything else. Or I'll make you wash and wax it."

Janet smirked, looking out the window. "Deal. I'd do that."

As he dropped her off, Ethan took note of Janet's house. It was old, and the yard was overgrown.

"Is your gardener on strike?" he joked.

Janet lowered her eyes, visibly jarred by the comment. Ethan immediately regretted it. He hadn't meant to embarrass her, but he could tell that he had. His heart sank.

"My mom said she'd get to it," Janet said, deflecting.

"Thank you. I'll see you around," she added as she stepped out.

Ethan gave an awkward wave as Janet disappeared around the side of the house.

CHAPTER 4

Ethan had just shut the Camaro door when he heard the snickering.

Three girls stood by the curb near the student drop-off loop, all of them in trendy jackets, their backpacks slung off one shoulder like fashion statements. He didn't know their names. They weren't in any of his classes, but he knew the type: loud, confident, and cruel in packs. Always in packs.

"Oh my God," the blonde one sneered. "Is that thing even street legal?"

"Looks like it needs a lethal injection," said the girl in glasses, wrinkling her nose as if the car actually smelled.

The third one, the one with glossy lips, added, "Who chooses to drive a rust bucket to school on purpose? Are you trying to cosplay poverty?"

Ethan didn't say anything. He'd rather avoid moments like this. He just kept walking, face flat, jaw tight.

The Camaro wasn't pretty—not yet. The paint was faded, the door mismatched, the back window whistled when the wind hit it. But it ran. It was his. It had been his dad's.

He kept walking and tried to pretend he hadn't heard them.

A familiar voice cut through the crowd like a knife.

"Oh, wow. Look—three girls with one personality trying to convince themselves they're not fake."

The girls froze and turned. Janet strode up like she owned the sidewalk—combat boots, messy bun, and her fully loaded sass mouth.

"You," the blonde scoffed, "weren't you just—"

Janet cut her off with a raised hand. "Nope. You've already hit your limit for stupid comments today."

She pointed at the blonde. "You look like you lost your shampoo. Your hair's greasy, and those eyebrows need attention. Might take pliers. Gross."

The blonde sputtered, but Janet had already moved on to the second girl.

"And you, Miss Fake Instagram Model. I wish those glasses were bigger, because we can still see that face."

Laughter burst out from a few nearby students. The third girl opened her mouth, but Janet stepped closer. Her voice turned calm—and sharp.

"And you, with the makeup. You need more. A lot more. Fix your face, because your personality isn't going to cut it."

Ethan watched the trio blink, speechless, the color draining from their over-blushed cheeks. A beat of silence passed.

Janet smiled sweetly. "Have a nice day."

The girls turned on their heels and scurried off, their exit nearly as dramatic as Janet's entrance.

Ethan stood frozen on the sidewalk, a half-smirk tugging at the corner of his mouth despite himself.

Janet turned to him, nonchalant. "You're welcome, grease monkey."

He raised an eyebrow. "I could've handled that."

"Oh, I'm sure," she said, leaning against the lockers, "by absorbing their insults into your soul and silently dying inside. Solid plan."

"I don't need saving." He shrugged.

"I know." Janet shrugged back. "I did it because I'm bored and those girls' faces annoy me."

Ethan gave a small laugh, shaking his head. "You're impossible."

"And you're the worst at comebacks," she said, flashing a grin. "Now come on, broody. I'll let you walk me to class."

Ethan tried going back to his routine—background student, head down, blend in. But he realized he missed having someone to talk to.

After school, the yelling started. It echoed across the quad like an alarm bell. A crowd had gathered near the gym steps. Shouts rang out, mostly boys, hyped on drama, phones already out, recording. Girls were pushing and spitting venom, their hands gesturing sharp and wild.

Ethan's stomach dropped when he saw her.

Janet.

She was in the center of it, defiant, wild-eyed, jaw set like a soldier waiting for someone to throw the first punch. It was the girls from that morning. One pushed, another screamed. Janet didn't back down. She never did. Her fists were clenched at her sides. She was shaking.

Ethan didn't think. He just moved. He shoved his way through, shouldering past gawkers and wannabe hype men. When he reached the middle, Janet was mid-step, ready to swing.

"Punch her!" someone shouted as the crowd egged on the carnage.

Ethan didn't say a word. He just wrapped his arms around her waist, turned, and lifted her over his shoulder.

"What the hell?! Put me down!" she shrieked.

"Not a chance," he grunted, slinging her like she weighed nothing.

She kicked her feet, uselessly. "You can't just kidnap people!"

"Evidently, I can," Ethan said.

The crowd parted for them, some laughing, others booing the lack of action. Ethan didn't care. He made a beeline for the Camaro, unlocked the door with one hand, and dropped her into the passenger seat before slamming it shut behind her.

She fumed in silence as he walked around and climbed into the driver's side.

"Unreal, Ethan Parker," she muttered. "You actually caveman'd me."

Ethan exhaled hard, still gripping the steering wheel. "You were about to throw hands over something you did for me."

Janet huffed. "They deserved it."

"I know they did."

Janet crossed her arms, staring straight ahead. For a moment, she didn't speak.

Then, softly, "They called me trash."

Ethan didn't respond. Not right away.

Janet rubbed her hands together. Her voice was flat now. "Not like it's new. But today it hit me differently. Maybe because I was already down on myself."

"Don't say that."

"Why not? I live in a crap house. My mom couldn't care less. I get in fights. I show up late or not at all. I'm loud and messed up, and no one expects anything from me except for fireworks. Trash kinda fits."

Ethan looked at her. Really looked.

There was something raw about her now. No smirk. No armor. Just a girl in combat boots with a cracked heart.

"They don't get to decide who you are," Ethan said quietly.

Janet let out a breath, half scoff, half sigh. "That sounds nice on paper."

"Then write it down," Ethan said. "Stick it somewhere. Read it when you're ready to believe it."

She turned her head and studied him for a beat. "You always talk like you're in a book."

"Because books make more sense than people." He shrugged.

That finally got a smile out of her. A small one. Tired, but real.

"Thanks," she said after a moment. "For whatever the hell that was."

Ethan nodded. "I was worried. I didn't want to see you hurt."

She leaned back against the seat, staring at the Camaro's cracked ceiling.

Janet shifted in the passenger seat, her knees pulled up to the dash, arms wrapped around them like a makeshift

shield. The adrenaline from the almost-fight had started to burn off, leaving a vulnerable silence in its place.

She stared out the windshield, her voice low. "You know what sucks the most? It's not that they called me trash. It's that… they could say it, and no one stopped them. No one said, 'Hey, back off.' Not even the ones who act cool with me during lunch or in class. I know people, Ethan. I talk to everyone. But no one's got my back."

Ethan kept his hands on the steering wheel, eyes forward. "Yeah. I get that."

Janet turned her head, studying his profile. "Do you?"

He nodded. "No one tries to fight me, sure. But not because they like me. It's because they don't notice me. I fly under the radar. I'm just... there."

"Like wallpaper," Janet pointed out.

"Exactly." He laughed softly, bitterly. "Nobody hates the wallpaper, but nobody talks to it either."

Janet rested her cheek against her knees. "That sounds... lonely."

Ethan shrugged. "It is. But it's quiet. Safe. I can be invisible, and no one expects anything from me. No disappointments. No drama."

Janet tilted her head, watching him. "You say that like it's a good thing."

"It's better than what you go through," Ethan said, finally glancing at her. "You're a firework show, and people want to see you go boom. But at least they see you."

Janet blinked, and for a second, she looked genuinely stunned. She didn't say anything, just picked at a loose thread on the cuff of her jacket.

Then, almost a whisper: "Sometimes I wish I was invisible. Just long enough to catch my breath."

Ethan offered her a soft smile. "We could trade for a day. You be the background guy. I'll be the wild gremlin."

She laughed. "You wouldn't survive an hour."

"Probably not. Too much talking."

Janet looked over at him, her eyes warmer now, a little less guarded. "You know, for someone who thinks no one notices him, you keep showing up when it counts."

"I didn't think," Ethan said. "I just saw you in the middle of that mess and... I couldn't let it happen."

"You always rescue damsels in combat boots?"

He smirked. "Only the ones that threaten to bite me."

Janet chuckled, then rested her head against the seat and closed her eyes. "I'm still mad, though."

"At them?"

"Yeah. But mostly at myself for letting it get to me. I should be better at pretending by now."

Ethan was quiet for a moment, then said gently, "You don't have to pretend with me."

Her eyes flicked open. She looked at him, something unreadable in her expression.

"I'll remember that," she said softly.

They sat in silence, the engine off, the outside world finally feeling like it couldn't reach them here. Not in this space. Not at this moment.

For the first time in a long time, for both, it didn't feel like they were completely alone.

After sitting for a while, just enjoying the quiet, Janet broke the silence. "I have an idea. Drive us to McDonald's. I'll buy us milkshakes."

"My mom does say ice cream fixes everything." Ethan started the Camaro.

CHAPTER 5

The next few days were... weird.

After Ethan had scooped Janet out of a full-blown fight and carried her off like some reluctant, flannel-wearing lioness, everything shifted. Not just because Janet had apparently decided she was now riding shotgun in his life. Things changed around them too. Eyes followed them in the halls. Whispers trailed behind their footsteps.

Ethan—usually invisible—felt like someone had flipped on a spotlight.

It didn't help that he'd started walking Janet to class. She never asked him to. She never asked for anything. But after that first day, when she slumped against the Camaro and said quietly, *"It was stupid, but it still hurt,"* Ethan hadn't been able to walk away.

So now, every day between periods, there they were. He was tall, quiet, and slightly irritated. She was unpredictable and sharp-tongued, practically daring people to say something.

Eventually, someone did.

They were crossing the quad, heading toward her English class and weaving between benches, when a sudden shoulder check knocked Ethan off-balance. He caught himself before falling, instinctively stepping in front of Janet.

Three boys stood in their way.

Football kids. Not varsity—JV, probably. Big enough to cause problems, dumb enough not to care.

"Well, well. If it isn't the junkyard prince and his trash-mouth princess," said the tallest, sneering. His letterman jacket stretched across his chest like it was barely surviving the pressure of his ego.

Janet stiffened behind Ethan.

"Real original, dork. What's next? A mom joke?"

But Ethan's eyes narrowed, assessing.

Behind the boys, just a few paces back, the three girls from before were waiting. Watching. The blonde one was cracking her knuckles. Glasses had her phone ready. The lip gloss girl wore that gleeful, pre-fight smile that told Ethan everything.

This wasn't about him.

It was a trap.

They wanted Janet.

Ethan took a step forward, his voice low.

"Out of our way."

He guided Janet toward the other side of the quad.

"You're not laying a finger on her."

The boy in the letterman jacket scoffed.

"Oh yeah? You gonna stop all of us? You think you're hard because you've got a rust bucket and a pissy little girlfriend?"

"She's not my—" Ethan began, but Janet cut him off.

"Actually, I'm nobody's anything. But if you want to test how fast I can kick a guy in skinny jeans, I'm ready."

Ethan glanced at her. She was shaking with fury, but also… fear. Not much. Just enough to make something inside him snap.

He stepped forward again, chest brushing the lead guy's.

"Back off," Ethan said calmly. "Walk away, or find out."

The boy's smirk twitched.

"What?"

"He means he'll knock your teeth out with one hand," Janet added helpfully. "And I'll rearrange the rest."

A pause.

The tension escalated—just long enough for a teacher to step out from a nearby door. Mr. Herrera. Science. Clueless and harmless, but an adult nonetheless.

The boys hesitated, exchanged looks, then peeled off.

"Not worth it," one muttered, though his glare said this wasn't over.

The girls didn't look quite so smug this time as they walked away, but Janet's eyes tracked them like a hawk.

When they were gone, she let out a breath.

"Thanks."

Ethan didn't answer. He just started walking.

She fell into step beside him.

"I don't need you to fight my battles."

"You didn't ask," Ethan replied, calm but not unkind. "But I'm not going to let someone hit you while I stand there."

Janet was quiet for a moment.

"You know they're not done, right? They're the kind of people who don't like to lose."

"Then let them come," Ethan said.

"You're not scared?"

He looked at her.

"Are you?"

She grinned, but it didn't quite reach her eyes.

"Just of what I'll do back."

They walked the rest of the way in silence, both of them aware something had shifted again.

This wasn't a joke anymore.

The school parking lot was buzzing when they stepped outside. Ethan could already see the silhouette of his Camaro, waiting like a loyal mutt at the far edge of the lot.

"Finally," he muttered. "Another day survived."

Janet walked a little ahead of him, her denim jacket slung over one shoulder, combat boots dragging more than usual. She glanced back and smirked.

"You know, if you didn't walk like an old man, we'd already be halfway home."

"I'm not the one who insisted on stopping to yell at a vending machine," Ethan said. "That Snickers bar is probably still stuck."

"It was a metaphor," she replied dryly. "For everything broken in this godforsaken school."

They were five feet from the Camaro when it happened.

The sound of fast footsteps was the only warning.

Ethan turned just as the first punch landed—sharp and low across his ribs. It knocked the breath out of him, but instinct kicked in. He twisted and caught a glimpse of the three JV boys from earlier, their smirks gone. All of them were swinging like they had something to prove.

"Janet!" he called, turning to check on her.

She was ready.

One of the girls launched herself at Janet, grabbing her hair and yanking her sideways. Janet hit the ground but came up like fire, swinging.

"You picked the wrong freakin' day!" she screamed, landing a sharp elbow into the blonde's jaw.

Ethan gritted his teeth. One of the boys charged him. This time, he didn't hold back.

He ducked the wild punch, stepped into the swing, and drove his fist into the kid's nose. There was a sharp crack, a cry of pain, and blood bloomed across the boy's upper lip.

"Come at me?" Ethan growled.

He turned just in time to take another hit across the face, splitting his lip. He tasted blood. A third boy tackled him, but Ethan used his weight to twist and slam the kid into the pavement.

He heard Janet's voice—angry, pained—and it hurt to hear her in trouble.

Ethan looked over and saw her on the ground now, right beside his car. Two of the girls had her pinned. She was still fighting, wild and kicking, but she was outnumbered.

He couldn't hit girls.

So, he did the only thing he could.

A very Ethan thing.

He ran full force into the fray, dropped down, and threw his body over Janet like a shield.

"Get off her!" he yelled, curling around her like a human barrier.

Fists landed. Feet too. Someone kicked him in the ribs. He took a knee to the spine. His arms tightened around Janet, pulling her head into his chest. He had put her between himself and the car, leaving his back to the attackers.

"Stay down," he whispered through gritted teeth. "I've got you."

Janet, stunned, stopped moving for a beat. His voice, soft and raw, cracked something open in her. She didn't say anything—just buried her face in his shirt, arms tight around his middle.

"Back up!" a voice roared.

Then came the whistles. Teacher voices. The fight broke up fast. Onlookers fled. Feet scattered. Someone grabbed Ethan's shoulder and pulled him upright. A security guard he didn't recognize shoved one of the boys to the ground and barked into a radio.

Ethan blinked through the pain. His vision swam.

Janet was sitting up now, her cheek red, lip bleeding, hair wild. But she was okay.

He turned to her, wincing as he knelt beside her.

"You good?" he asked hoarsely.

Janet stared at him, her voice low and shaking. "You let them hit you."

He shrugged, then winced. "I didn't know what else to do."

Her eyes flicked to the bruises blooming across his face, the blood on his shirt, and something unfamiliar passed through her—a mix of guilt, awe, and the strange comfort of feeling safe.

She touched his busted lip gently.

"You're an idiot," she whispered, and wrapped her arms around his neck.

Ethan smirked. "So I've been told."

Teachers barked about detentions and suspensions, but for the moment, Ethan and Janet stayed there in the parking lot, surrounded by chaos and broken pride, wrapped in a silence heavier than anything the school could hand down.

Because for the first time in a long time, they both had someone in their corner.

CHAPTER 6

The walls of the Vice Principal's office were the color of disappointment—off-white and stained with years of bad behavior. Ethan sat in the plastic chair, one eye swelling shut, his knuckles scraped and bruised. Beside him, Janet slouched with her arms crossed, her boot tapping against the tile in a rapid, angry rhythm.

Across the hall, the door to the principal's office opened and closed like a revolving gate. Parents arrived, voices low and tight. One by one, the other students from the fight were ushered out with tissues, lecture faces, and even hugs.

No one came for Ethan.

No one came for Janet.

Janet chewed the inside of her cheek. "You know what's funny?" she said, voice hushed.

Ethan raised an eyebrow. "What?"

"They're in there talking about us. Making decisions. Writing it all down like they were standing in the fight. They weren't there." She looked over at him. "They're probably deciding if we're animals or just screwups."

Ethan exhaled and rested his head back against the wall. "Guess we're both. Guess we shouldn't have defended ourselves."

Janet looked at him. "Watch. They'll see me as the animal. You'll be the poor kid who got in the way."

Before he could respond, the Vice Principal's door creaked open. Ethan and Janet looked to see who it was.

"Ethan Parker?" Mr. Lennox said, clipboard in hand. "Come in."

Ethan started to stand, but Janet was already moving.

"I'm coming too," she said.

Lennox blinked. "Janet, no. I need to speak with him alone."

"No," she replied, steady and firm. "You're not going to twist things. He doesn't know how this works."

"I do fine on my own," Ethan muttered, but she ignored him.

Lennox pinched the bridge of his nose. "Fine. Both of you. Let's get this over with."

They stepped into the office. It smelled like printer toner and sour coffee. The blinds were drawn. The manila folders stacked on the desk might as well have been case files.

Mr. Lennox sat down with a sigh.

"So. We couldn't reach either of your parents. Ethan, you're eighteen, so we don't legally have to notify your mother. Janet..." He frowned. "No one answered at your home. Again."

Janet shrugged, but Ethan caught the flinch in her jaw. Her arms tightened across her chest. He wondered about that—something wasn't right.

Lennox leaned forward, breaking into Ethan's thoughts. "I've spoken to the others. According to their statements, Janet instigated the fight. The boys only stepped in when Ethan interfered."

"That's bull," Ethan started, but Janet placed a hand on his arm.

"They're lying," she said coolly. "But of course they are. That's what scared kids do. They make up stories and hope you'll buy them."

Lennox tapped his pen against the desk. "I'm not really interested in who threw the first punch. This isn't about heroics. It's about choices. You both participated in a violent confrontation on school property."

Ethan clenched his jaw. *Once again, they didn't care about the why.*

"So, what's the verdict?" Janet asked. "Are we expelled or just banished for a while?"

"Ten days' suspension," Lennox said. "Both of you. Effective immediately."

Janet leaned back and let out a low whistle. "Wow. Double digits. You really threw the book at us, didn't you."

"I suggest you use the time to reflect," Lennox replied. "Maybe even grow up."

Ethan stood slowly. "We done?"

Lennox didn't answer. He just scribbled a note on the clipboard and handed each of them a yellow copy of the suspension form.

As they walked out of the office, Janet folded hers into a paper airplane and tossed it in the trash. Ethan glanced over at her.

"You didn't have to come in with me," he said quietly.

Janet looked up at him, fierce and stubborn. "Yeah. I did. You stood up for me."

The student parking lot was empty now, quiet except for the occasional hum of cars passing on the road in front of the school. Ethan sat behind the wheel of his Camaro, staring out through the cracked windshield like it might hold answers. Janet sat in the passenger seat, legs pulled up, boots dusting the faded dashboard.

Neither of them spoke for a long time.

The silence wasn't awkward. It was comfortable, like an old hoodie.

Ethan finally shifted in his seat, eyes on the rearview mirror. "Ten days off," he said, trying to keep it light. "Guess that's a win."

Janet gave a dry laugh. "Yeah, sure. A vacation with a side of character assassination."

He smiled faintly, but the bruise on his cheekbone twinged, pulling his expression into a wince.

"You okay?" she asked, turning to him. Her voice had lost its usual edge.

"I've been better," he said. "But I'm fine. Just… pissed."

"At them?" she asked.

"Yeah," he muttered. "And at myself. For not seeing it coming. I knew they were after you. Should've walked you out sooner."

Janet stared at him. "You're seriously mad that you didn't protect me faster?"

He looked over at her, brow furrowed. "You don't get it."

Janet shook her head. "No, you don't get it. No one's ever done that. What you did—throwing yourself on top of me like some kind of human riot shield. Who does that?"

"I didn't think. I just… couldn't let them hurt you," Ethan said quietly. "I've seen people take hits and pretend it doesn't bother them, but I've never seen someone take as many as you and still get up swinging."

Janet bit her lip. Her voice went small, like it wasn't used to being soft. "I'm not used to anyone worrying about me. Not in a real way. Usually, it's just some teacher saying I'm a 'concern' or people pitying me from a distance."

Ethan looked down at his hands. "I guess I just didn't want to be another person watching."

Janet let that settle between them, her eyes tracing the edges of the dash. "You know what scared me more than the fight?"

He looked up. "What?"

"When you covered me. I wanted to fight back. I always fight back. But you stopped me, and I didn't hate it. I felt… safe."

Ethan turned slightly toward her. "I didn't mean to make you feel powerless."

"You didn't," she said. "You made me feel… like someone had my back for once. Like I wasn't alone in the fire."

Ethan exhaled slowly. "I know what it's like to be alone. I've been invisible most of my life. It's easier not to get hurt when no one sees you."

Janet gave a sad smile. "I think I did the opposite. Made sure everyone saw me, even if it was for the wrong reasons. I was loud so no one saw that I was scared."

Ethan's fingers tapped the steering wheel absently. "You still scared?"

Janet nodded once. "Yeah. But not right now."

They sat in that moment, not needing to be anything more than what they were—two bruised, misunderstood souls in a beat-up Camaro with the windows cracked and the world quiet around them.

"I have an idea," Janet said suddenly.

Ethan raised an eyebrow. "Like what?"

Janet started giving directions. Ethan started the car. The rumble filled the silence, grounding them both. She leaned her head back against the seat, smiling at the ceiling. He didn't know where they were going, not yet, but for the first time, he wasn't going alone.

Ethan drove with the windows down. Janet leaned out slightly, her hair whipping around her face like wild ribbons.

"Left on the next dirt road," she called out, pointing ahead with a finger smudged in permanent marker doodles. "Trust me."

"That's what people say right before they get you killed," Ethan muttered, but he turned anyway.

The Camaro bounced down the gravel path, trees leaning close over the road like they were eavesdropping. After a few twists and turns, the trail opened into a hidden clearing, a pool of water tucked beneath an old, craggy bluff. A narrow waterfall spilled down the rock face into a wide, shallow basin. The sun hit the water just right, scattering light like loose coins across the surface.

Ethan parked under an oak and stepped out, stunned into silence.

Janet hopped out barefoot, shoes slung over her shoulder. "Well?" she said with a crooked grin. "Not bad for trash, huh?"

Ethan shook his head, lips twitching. "Not bad at all."

They climbed down the boulders to the water's edge. Ethan sat to take off his shoes and socks. The water was shin-deep and clear as glass. Janet waded in first, her gasp sharp as the cold gripped her ankles.

"Holy crap, it's freezing!" she laughed, hopping from foot to foot. "Come on in, tough guy."

Ethan rolled his eyes but stepped in carefully. The cold was immediate—numbing, bracing, and somehow perfect. Janet splashed a wave of water straight at his chest.

He blinked, soaked, then gave her a slow, devilish look. "You sure you want to start this?"

"You scared?" she taunted.

He lunged, sending a tidal wave of water her way. She shrieked and ran, but the basin only let her get so far. They chased and splashed, laughing until they were breathless, soaked head to toe, the bruises on their skin forgotten for a while.

At one point, Ethan paused, water dripping from his curls, his hands on his knees. "Okay... truce," he panted.

"Coward," Janet said, but her voice was warm.

They stood in the pool, catching their breath, water swirling around their legs. Janet looked down at her reflection, then over at Ethan.

"I used to come here when things got bad at home," she said softly. "Figured if I had one place that was mine, it meant something."

Ethan nodded. "I get that. I have a stretch of road I drive sometimes. Just to drive. Like maybe if I go far enough, I won't feel stuck anymore."

Janet looked at him, serious now. "I'm glad you brought me here today."

"You brought me," he reminded her.

"Yeah... but you stayed."

They stood in silence, the sound of the waterfall folding over them like a blanket. For once, the world wasn't so heavy. The fight, the suspension, the bruises—it all felt like another life.

"I don't know what this is," Janet said, looking at him. "But... I don't hate it."

"Me neither," Ethan said.

The sun dipped lower in the sky, and the cold water gave them goosebumps, but neither of them moved.

"We don't have any towels," Ethan noted, ever practical.

"Not an issue." Janet hopped onto the hood and lay back against the windshield.

Ethan joined her.

The metal of the Camaro's hood was warm beneath their damp clothes as they lay side by side, staring up at the sky. The late afternoon sun filtered through the oak leaves, broken clouds drifting like lazy ships above them.

Janet's hair fanned out behind her, drying into chaotic waves. Ethan folded his hands behind his head, elbows wide, a quiet peace softening his usually wary eyes.

"This is what life should feel like," Ethan said.

"Okay," Janet said, her voice unusually calm. "Serious question."

Ethan turned his head slightly. "Hit me."

"What do you want? Like, from life. For real."

He was quiet for a moment—long enough for the wind to stir before he answered.

"I guess... I want something that feels like mine. Not handed down. Not expected. Just something that makes me feel like I matter. Like I'm not invisible."

Janet's brow furrowed. "You're not invisible."

"I am to everyone else," he said, still staring at the clouds. "Even in a room full of people. I blend in. I don't make waves. I don't disappoint anyone that way. But... it's lonely."

Janet rolled to her side, propping herself up on her elbow. "You're not built to be invisible, Ethan. You carried me out of a fight like a damn action hero."

He smirked. "Only because you were about to throw a trash can."

"Fair," she said with a grin.

Ethan turned his head, meeting her eyes. "What about you?"

She flopped back onto her back and blew out a breath. "Honestly, I didn't know until recently, but I want to feel safe. Like, actually safe. Like I can let my guard down and not get kicked for it. I want to be... wanted."

They let the wind answer for a moment, whistling softly through the trees.

Then Janet suddenly sat up straight, eyes wide.

"I have an idea!" she shouted.

Ethan groaned, half-laughing. "Oh no. That's never a good thing when you say it like that."

"No, listen," she said, bouncing slightly on the hood. "We've got ten whole days off. No school, no teachers, no jerks trying to jump us in the parking lot."

"Temporarily," he reminded her.

"Exactly. Temporary freedom. So, let's use it. Let's hang out."

"Like... every day?" Ethan asked.

"Why not?" Janet shrugged, a smile tugging at her lips. "We've already been through the hard part together, right?"

Ethan looked up at her, a slow smile spreading across his face. "So, what, we're just going to spend our suspension being... friends?"

Janet tilted her head. "Sure. Friends with bruises. Maybe even a plan."

He laughed, shaking his head. "You're trouble."

"You love it," she said.

Ethan thought to himself, maybe he did.

"What time do you want to pick me up?" Janet asked.

CHAPTER 7

Ethan blocked the sun with his hand. It was still early as he pulled up in front of Janet's place. She was already outside, sitting on the curb with a backpack slung over one shoulder, legs crossed, and a look of mild surprise on her face when she saw the Camaro.

"You're early," she said, standing and brushing gravel from her jeans.

"I wanted to get here before you had time to plan my demise," Ethan replied with a half-smile.

"I wouldn't do that. Suspension changes a girl," she teased, tossing her bag into the back seat. "Let's go, my personal Uber."

The ride was quiet, not awkward. Just that kind of easy silence that only happens when two people are starting to understand each other.

When they pulled into Ethan's driveway, Janet tilted her head slightly, taking in the modest one-story house, the ivy crawling across the porch, and a wind chime swaying in the breeze.

Inside, the smell of bacon and eggs wrapped around them like a hug. Ethan's mom stood at the stove, flipping pancakes. She turned as they entered, eyebrows lifting in surprise.

"This must be Janet," she said, wiping her hands on a towel and offering a warm smile. "You're just in time for breakfast."

Janet hesitated for a moment, clearly unused to this kind of welcome, but recovered quickly. "Smells better than the cafeteria."

They sat down, Janet cautious at first, not quite comfortable enough to be herself. Gradually, she started to relax under the charm of Ethan's mom. She noticed how gracious she was, chatting easily as they ate. It felt

unfamiliar, like a scene from a corny family sitcom. Janet even laughed—a real laugh that caught her off guard.

After breakfast, Ethan's mom grabbed her purse and kissed him on the cheek. "Don't burn down the kitchen. I'll be home late. Be good."

The door clicked shut. Janet stood and stretched. "Your mom is... so sweet."

"She's kind of the best," Ethan said, stacking plates.

They moved to the kitchen sink without discussing it, slipping into a quiet rhythm. He washed, she dried. She elbowed him when he tried to stack wet plates, and he flicked suds at her in return.

"So," Janet said, tossing the towel over her shoulder, "what now?"

"You still owe me a car wash," Ethan said with a grin.

Janet planted her feet like a petulant child. "I did not agree to manual labor when I got suspended."

Ethan shrugged. "Too late. I distinctly remember you saying you would do it."

In the driveway, Ethan hauled out a bucket, soap, and sponge. Janet helped—reluctantly at first—but within minutes, she was soaking the Camaro, spraying Ethan's boots by "accident," and humming along with the music coming from the garage speaker.

As they scrubbed and rinsed, Ethan caught himself looking at the car more than usual. His voice dropped a little.

"This car always reminds me of my dad," he said. "It was his project car before he got sick."

Janet paused, sponge still dripping. "I remember."

"He died two years ago. Cancer." Ethan's voice stayed steady, but his jaw tightened. "We were supposed to fix it up together. It's not much to look at, but... I see more than a car."

Janet leaned against the hood, her voice softer. "It's beautiful. Even if the radio only plays classic rock."

Ethan chuckled, but the laugh faded quickly. "I guess I had to grow up fast after that. Be the man of the house. Be... boring and responsible."

"You're not boring," Janet said. "You're solid. Do you know how rare that is?"

He glanced at her, surprised.

Janet looked away, drying her hands on her jeans. "I never had that. My mom's always gone, my dad's just a name on paper. People know of me, but no one really knows me."

Ethan mirrored her on the opposite side of the hood. "That's how I feel. Except... I like hiding. It's safer."

Janet gave him a sideways glance, half-smiling. "Hard to stay hidden if you're hanging out with me."

"I know," Ethan said, lightly touching the fading bruise on his face.

Janet nodded. "I meant it earlier. You're lucky, you know? You've got a home, a mom who cooks breakfast, a car that has stories. That brand of boring... it's gold."

They stood in silence, the Camaro gleaming between them, water glinting on its curves like morning dew. The hose hissed softly where it lay coiled on the driveway. At that moment, Ethan didn't feel quite so alone. And for the first time, Janet didn't feel quite so lost.

Back inside, Janet dropped her backpack on the floor. "I have an idea."

Ethan raised an eyebrow. "I kind of thought you would."

She pulled out the paperback he'd started reading to her in detention.

"Don't be mad. I know I shouldn't have taken it. But I need to know how it ends. Will you read it to me?"

Ethan smiled, relieved. "On the scale of 'Janet ideas,' this one's pretty mild."

They sat down on the sofa. Ethan's voice was low and steady as he began to read. It felt like a hug she hadn't realized she needed. Janet listened intently, not just to the story, but to him. After a while, she lay her head in his lap. It surprised him, but he didn't miss a beat.

Janet was like a cat. She took what she wanted but somehow made Ethan feel lucky to give it. He switched the book to his other hand and rested the other lightly on her stomach. She closed her eyes. If she were a cat, this would be the moment she purred.

When Janet opened her eyes again, the room was dark. She was in a bed, disoriented. Her hair clung to her face in wrinkled strands, and her skin bore faint creases from the sheets.

She heard voices down the hall and followed them to the kitchen, where Ethan and his mom were setting the table. His mom had brought home takeout.

"Well, hello, Sleeping Beauty," she said, smiling. "How are you feeling?"

Janet blinked at her, still groggy.

"Ethan, get our guest some water," his mom said gently. "You must've been tired, little lady."

"I guess I dozed off," Janet mumbled, rubbing her eyes.

"Yeah," Ethan said, "I marked the page where I think you fell asleep. But I'm not totally sure."

Janet glanced at him. "How did I get into bed?"

"I carried you like a little baby, but I was a total gentleman," Ethan said with mock pride.

She rolled her eyes. "You're ridiculous."

"Let's eat," his mom said.

After dinner, Ethan drove her home. The air was cooler now, and the Camaro rumbled softly beneath them.

When they pulled up to her place, Janet lingered.

"You'll come get me tomorrow, right?"

Ethan nodded. "I guess I could."

She smiled—not a smirk, but something softer. "Good."

She got out, shutting the door behind her with a reverent click.

Ethan was feeling content the next day as he pulled up to Janet's place.

He had just unlocked the passenger door when Janet slid into the seat and gave him a serious look.

"I have an idea," she said, buckling in.

Ethan gave her a wary glance. "That phrase is becoming dangerous."

Janet smiled. "I was just thinking... what if I stayed at your house? Like, overnight. Just until our suspension is over."

He blinked. "Really?"

"Yesterday was... maybe the best day of my life," she admitted, eyes straight ahead. "But when I got home, it was just this cold, empty house in the middle of nowhere. Creepy quiet. I couldn't sleep. It felt so... I don't know... lonely."

Ethan hesitated. "I mean, I'm fine with it. But we'll have to ask my mom."

Janet nodded. "I figured that. But I wanted to ask you first."

Mrs. Parker didn't even blink when they brought it up at breakfast. She just stirred her coffee, her eyes soft behind her glasses.

"If her mom's okay with it, then I don't see why not."

Janet quickly replied, "She said she didn't care."

And just like that, Janet stayed.

Every day of their suspension felt like a stolen summer. Janet had a seemingly endless list of ideas for adventure. They started at the playground, climbing over old metal equipment like they were kids again—jumping from swings, daring each other up the wobbly rope tower.

They spent time at the park. Janet insisted they climb the tallest rocks, where the wind pulled at their clothes and the sky felt closer. They brought crackers and fed ducks at the edge of a still pond. Janet gave every duck a name.

"That one's Chandler. That's Ross. That grumpy one is Monica. She's judging us."

"Monica looks more like Karen," Ethan said.

They laughed until their cheeks hurt.

Near the end of the week, they hiked through Jackson's Wildlife Preserve. It was a beautiful trail, where massive oaks towered overhead, draped in thick vines.

Janet breathed heavily. "There were so many twists to that trail."

Janet spotted a set of railroad tracks that seemed to lead toward the parking lot. "We should walk along the rails."

At one point, the track crossed a river—a high, railed bridge.

"I have an idea. Let's jump off the old railroad bridge," Janet suggested.

Ethan looked at the drop. "You mean, like... on purpose?"

"It's not that high. And I've seen people do it before."

She took his hand and guided him to the top of the cement pylons holding up the bridge. "Come on. Don't overthink it."

They stood beside the track on the cement platform, looking down. Water shimmered far below. Suddenly, the tracks began to tremble, and they both knew a train was coming. The sharp sound of the whistle confirmed it.

"Janet," Ethan said nervously.

"We can't climb back now," she said, calm but urgent.

The train's horn blasted as it started across the bridge. The vibration pulsed through their feet. The jump wasn't a dare anymore; it was a necessity.

Janet took his hand. "Together? Now!"

They leaped.

The air roared past them, then came the rush of water. Cold and all-consuming, it swallowed them whole. It felt much longer than it was—Ethan's lungs began to ache, desperate for air. Just when he hit his limit, they surfaced, coughing and laughing and yelling like maniacs.

Ethan was wide-eyed, breathless. "That was insane!"

"You loved it," Janet said, grinning as she floated beside him.

The rush, the risk, the way the world disappeared for a moment—it made him feel alive.

On the way home, Ethan pulled into the empty parking lot of an abandoned warehouse.

"Do you want to drive? I was thinking... you're seventeen. We should get you a license." He wasn't being impulsive; he was being practical.

"I don't know. What if I break your car?" Janet was nervous—not out of fear, but because she cared what Ethan thought.

They spent hours practicing. Janet grew more confident, more empowered. She felt honored that Ethan trusted her with something that meant so much to him.

The days blurred together in the best way. At night, they'd hang out in the living room, watching movies or reading together until one of them fell asleep mid-sentence. Ethan gave Janet his room, and he took the couch.

On the last night of suspension, they sat on the roof of Ethan's garage, legs dangling over the edge, the stars spread out above them.

Janet leaned back on her palms. "Tomorrow, we have to go back."

"Yeah," Ethan said quietly.

"Are you nervous?" she asked.

Ethan thought about it. "I'm not really nervous. I mean... yeah, a little. But I wish we could stay like this."

Janet tilted her head. "Yeah."

He looked at her. "This week was perfect. I don't want it to end."

Janet was quiet for a second. Then she said, "It doesn't have to. Not all of it, anyway."

Ethan smiled. "You've got another idea, don't you?"

She bumped her shoulder against him. "Of course I do."

And under the stars, with bruised knees and sunburned noses, they didn't feel like two kids on suspension. They felt like something else—something more natural than whatever waited for them in the school halls.

CHAPTER 8

Ethan picked up Janet that morning, just like he had every day for the past two weeks, but this time the air in the car felt heavier. Quiet. Not nervous—just bracing.

Neither of them said it out loud, but they both knew today was going to be rough.

They didn't share any classes, which only made it worse. Alone in separate halls, separate rooms, they had to face their return on their own.

Ethan didn't even make it to first period before someone tossed a crumpled gum wrapper at his back and muttered,

"Trash Man returns."

In his second class, he did the usual—grabbed the trash bin and headed to the hallway like the teacher asked.

He was halfway to the door when someone coughed,

"You sure are good at taking out trash."

Snickers followed. A few desks tapped in rhythm, like they were encouraging it. The teacher looked up, sighed, and said nothing.

Ethan clenched his fists, dumped the bin, and returned to his seat. He didn't speak for the rest of the class.

Across the school, Janet was facing it too.

Girls stared at her like she was a walking scandal. They didn't whisper. They made sure their comments were loud enough for her to hear.

"Did you hear she's living with him?"

"Bet she wears his clothes since she can't afford her own."

"He probably just feels sorry for her."

Janet didn't react. She didn't even glance their way. But every word hit like a stone to the ribs. By lunchtime, she felt like she couldn't breathe.

They found each other by the tree behind the gym—the only place no one else wanted to sit.

Ethan dropped beside her without a word. Janet unwrapped her sandwich, stared at it, then dropped it back into the bag.

"I hate this place," she said softly.

Ethan didn't speak for a moment. Then he said, "I didn't think it would be this bad."

She looked at him. "They don't even care what's true. They just want something nasty to say."

"Every time I walk past a group of guys, it's the same thing. Trash man. Dumpster couple. Freak show."

Janet let out a bitter laugh. "Someone called me your charity project."

Ethan shook his head slowly. "Why does everyone think we owe them an explanation?"

"Because they're bored," she said flatly. "And we gave them something new to chew on."

By Wednesday, Ethan got another note stuffed into his locker:

"Trash man can't find any better. Hope she came with a receipt."

He crumpled the note into his fist and shoved it deep into his hoodie pocket. He didn't even tell Janet.

He couldn't stand to see her face fall again.

That afternoon, they sat on the edge of the field near the bleachers. No one else was around.

"I don't want to come back tomorrow," Janet said.

"I don't either," Ethan replied.

She leaned her head on his shoulder. "I didn't think I'd ever say this, but… I miss suspension."

Ethan gave a hollow laugh. "Same. I'd take rock climbing and feeding ducks over this any day."

"I thought I could tough it out," she whispered. "But I feel like I'm drowning."

Ethan reached over and held her hand. "We're drowning together, at least."

Janet squeezed his hand. "Not sure that helps."

"Me neither."

They stayed there, pressed against the edge of the world, clinging to the only thing that made sense anymore.

It was late afternoon, and the hallway outside the counselor's office was deserted, echoing faintly with the sound of Ethan's shoes and the sharper click of Janet's combat boots. They had just dodged another tense moment in the hall—glares from students, muttered comments, and a folder that had mysteriously landed on the floor near them again.

Ethan rubbed the back of his neck, jaw clenched. "How many more days of this do we have to deal with?"

Janet didn't answer. She had slowed down, her eyes drifting across the bulletin board beside the office. A tattered brochure was half-pinned at the bottom corner. She tugged it loose and scanned the cover.

Independent Study Program: Learn at Your Own Pace, from Anywhere.

Her eyes lit up. "I have an idea," she said, holding it up like a golden ticket.

Ethan tilted his head warily. "That phrase should come with a warning label."

She waved the paper in his face. "No, seriously, look. It says we can do the rest of our classes online. Work from home, no crowds, no fights, no drama. We could actually finish high school without... all this."

Ethan took the brochure from her, scanning the details. "You think they'd let us? After the suspension and everything?"

"Why wouldn't they?" Janet shrugged. "We're passing. We're not the problem. The school just doesn't know what to do with people like us. People who don't fit into their cute little boxes."

Ethan ran a thumb along the edge of the paper. The idea of waking up, learning at home, doing schoolwork in peace… it sounded almost too good to be real.

"We should at least ask," Janet said, nudging him with her elbow. "I mean, come on. What's more rebellious than quietly disappearing from the circus?"

Ethan chuckled. "And just like that, your most dangerous idea yet is actually... smart."

Janet grinned. "Scary, right?"

That night, Ethan sat hunched at the dining room table, laptop open, a half-empty mug of hot chocolate growing cold beside him. The soft tap of keys filled the quiet house as he read every page of the Independent Study Program site—requirements, deadlines, expectations. It was all there. It could work.

"We can do this!" Janet squealed.

He leaned back, exhaling slowly, then hit "Print."

The printer in the corner came to life, buzzing and whirring as it spat out the necessary documents. Ethan collected the pages, grabbed a pen, and sat back down. The form asked for a parent or guardian signature… but not for him. At eighteen, he could sign his own future.

He scrawled his name across the line with quiet finality.

Janet filled out hers too, except for her mother's signature.

The next morning, the Camaro's engine grumbled as Ethan pulled up outside Janet's house. She was already in the passenger seat, her form clutched in one hand.

"Can I borrow a pen?" she asked, climbing out of the car.

"Yeah. You just need a signature," Ethan said.

Janet nodded and flipped through the pages. "Okay, okay. Got it."

He handed her a pen. "Will your mom go for it?"

She didn't answer right away. She just raised her brows, took the pen, and said, "Wait here."

She disappeared inside in a flash, the heavy front door creaking shut behind her. Ethan leaned back in his seat, watching the porch through the windshield, tapping his fingers lightly on the wheel.

Exactly two minutes later, she reappeared with the signed form in hand and a crooked little smile on her face.

"All set," she said, climbing back in and fastening her seatbelt.

Ethan glanced at the paper. The signature was scribbled fast and messy. No fanfare. No hesitation.

"You're serious about this? We're really going to do it."

Janet looked out the window, her voice softer now. "Let's get it done."

Ethan nodded once, started the engine, and pulled away from the curb. The Camaro rolled forward toward something they hadn't expected: freedom.

The front office smelled like floor polish and fading optimism. Ethan held the forms in one hand. Janet's fingers were laced through the fingers of his other. She was twitching with her usual energy. They stood side by side, facing the principal's desk.

Principal Dawes folded his hands and leaned forward. "Now, listen. Independent study isn't a vacation.

It's real work. No teachers chasing you down. No make-up tests. No prom. You miss out on a lot of what makes senior year… well, senior year."

"We know," Ethan said calmly. He was taller than Mr. Dawes, even though the older man had the bigger chair. But it wasn't his height that made the words land. It was the quiet certainty behind them.

Janet smirked. "Prom wasn't exactly on my bucket list."

Dawes turned to her. "And you, Ms. Rhodes. Frankly, I worry this is just you running away."

Janet's jaw set. "I'm not running. I'm choosing. There's a difference."

"She knows what she's doing," Ethan added.

He slid the forms across the desk. "We've already talked to the district. The deadlines, the requirements—it's all within policy."

Dawes studied them both, sighed, and finally reached for a pen. He signed Ethan's file, then Janet's.

"Alright," he said, setting the pen down like it weighed more than it should. "You're officially off the roster."

Janet smiled. "Cool."

The sunlight hit them as they stepped back into the parking lot, like they'd just pulled off a prison break.

Janet raised her arms in triumph. "We're free!"

Ethan grinned despite himself. "Don't jinx it."

She bumped his shoulder with hers. "I have an idea. We should celebrate."

"Oh yeah? With what?"

She turned to him with wide eyes and a mischievous grin. "Ice cream. Duh. That's what people do when they make life-changing decisions."

Ten minutes later, they were parked outside Dairy Queen, sitting on the hood of the Camaro with waffle cones in hand. Ethan had gone for vanilla—of course he played it safe. Janet, naturally, ordered chocolate peanut butter.

"You know," Ethan said between bites, "this is the weirdest, best day I've had in months."

Janet swung her legs lazily. "We're doing life our way."

He looked at her cone, now dripping onto her hand. "You're melting."

Janet licked it messily and shrugged. "Worth it."

And for once, Ethan didn't feel like the invisible kid. And Janet didn't feel like the girl always on the edge of a fight.

For the first time, they felt like two people who just might have figured out their own way forward.

CHAPTER 9

Each morning, Ethan and Janet woke up, ate breakfast, and settled at the kitchen table with their laptops open, notebooks sprawled, and earbuds in.

Janet had even started writing her answers in complete sentences. She was enjoying learning; it felt different now that she had chosen it for herself.

"I feel like a real student," she joked one afternoon, holding up a biology quiz with a proud C+.

"You're practically an academic weapon," Ethan replied with a grin. He took her quiz and hung it on the fridge.

"I'm proud of you," Ethan said, and he meant it.

They made it a routine: study during the day, play in the afternoon, and hang out at night. Ethan had been sleeping

on the living room couch the entire time, curled up in a pile of pillows and blankets.

But one night, after the dishes were done and the house was quiet, Ethan asked the question that had been eating at him for days.

"Janet," he said gently. "Where's your mom?"

Janet didn't answer right away. She sat back on the couch, arms folded tight. Then her jaw began to tremble.

Ethan put his arm around her.

"I don't know," she said finally, her voice cracking. "She's been gone for months."

Ethan blinked. "What do you mean, gone?"

"She left," Janet said. "Disappeared. It's not the first time. Usually she comes back, but this time… she hasn't. I tried calling. Nothing."

She paused, then added, "I've been selling stuff in the house to buy food. Pawned my tablet. Sold the microwave. Stopped paying for water. Electricity was next."

Ethan didn't know what to say. He just sat there with her, letting the truth settle between them.

"I didn't want to tell you," she whispered. "Or your mom. I didn't want to wreck this."

"You can't wreck anything," Ethan said. "You're not trash. You're just surviving, like the rest of us. You could have told me, but I'm glad you told me now." He kissed her on the top of her head. "It's going to be okay."

Later that night, Ethan and Janet told his mom everything.

The next morning, his mom quietly rearranged her home office. She moved her desk into the corner and brought out an old bed frame and mattress from the garage. New sheets, a fresh pillow, and a folded quilt waited on top.

When Janet came in, his mom just said, "You're not a guest anymore. You're family. You deserve your own room."

Janet stared at the bed like it might disappear if she blinked. Then she burst into tears.

Ethan's mom hugged her, and Janet clung like a kid who hadn't been held in years.

That evening, Janet stood in the doorway of her new room, running her fingers over the edge of the desk. She looked up when Ethan leaned against the frame.

"You okay?" he asked.

She nodded, eyes glassy. "I don't know what I did to deserve you guys."

Ethan shrugged. "You were there when I needed someone. You stayed. You didn't run."

"I didn't have anywhere to run," she said.

"Doesn't matter. You stayed," Ethan said. "And I'm glad you live here. Not just because it's easier. Because I like having you here."

Janet smiled. Quiet, tired, but real. "Thanks for not giving up on me."

Ethan looked back toward the hallway. "You wanna work on history or watch a dumb movie?"

"Let's do both," Janet said. "Multitask like geniuses."

They sat on the floor with popcorn and textbooks, learning about economics while quoting old movies and quizzing each other with candy as prizes.

By the end of the fifth week, Janet had a toothbrush in the bathroom, a drawer in the dresser, and a favorite mug in the kitchen cabinet.

She still called it Ethan's house, but her routines made it clear she lived there now. Mornings started with quiet shuffling in the kitchen — Ethan's mom humming to herself, pouring a cup of coffee for herself and cocoa for Janet. Ethan dragged himself in twenty minutes later, hair messy, hoodie half on, mumbling something about needing three more hours of sleep.

Janet had started setting the table. No one asked her to. She just did it, like it was her kitchen too.

Ethan's mom had taken to calling her "J," and somewhere between Tuesday and Thursday, she asked Janet if she wanted to come shopping.

"Just a few things," she said casually. "You're making do with what you've got, but I know there's stuff you're missing."

Janet hesitated. "Like what?"

"Well, socks that match. A jacket that isn't just Ethan's sweatshirt. And probably a brush that wasn't bought at a gas station."

Janet laughed — the kind of laugh that caught her by surprise.

They spent the afternoon drifting between stores. Nothing fancy, just simple, solid things. A set of pajamas. A pair of jeans that actually fit. Shampoo she picked out for the scent.

When they got home, Janet tried on the sweater Ethan's mom insisted she needed. Soft. Forest green. It made her eyes look brighter.

Ethan noticed that part.

"You look… like you," he said awkwardly.

Janet rolled her eyes but smiled anyway. "What does that even mean?"

"Like you're not hiding anymore."

Evenings took on a rhythm. Dinner together. Whoever cooked didn't have to clean. Janet had taken a liking to grilled cheese at night, and she made a mess doing it, but always laughed when Ethan's mom teased her about buttering the counter more than the bread.

After dinner, they'd finish schoolwork at the kitchen table. Ethan's mom worked in her now-corner office just a few feet away, sometimes chiming in with the answer to a math problem or an explanation of an economic principle. She said she liked the sound of them working. It made the house feel alive again.

Sometimes, when Janet stayed up late reading, Ethan's mom would poke her head in and say, "Lights out, young lady." Not sharp. Not commanding. Just warm. Parental.

Janet liked the attention — attention she didn't have to fight for.

One night, Ethan found Janet in the laundry room folding towels. She had earbuds in and didn't hear him come in.

"You know you don't have to do chores," he said.

"I know," she replied, not looking up. "But I want to. I like this... I don't know. Feeling useful. Being part of it."

Ethan leaned against the doorframe. "You are part of it."

She stopped folding for a second and looked at him.

"Do you think it's okay that I like this so much?" she asked softly. "Like... it's not mine, but I want it to be."

Ethan didn't hesitate. "Yeah. I think that's the best part."

That night, Janet wrote in a notebook she hadn't shown anyone. A kind of journal. Just a few lines:

Things I don't want to lose:

The green sweater.

The sound of bacon crackling in the morning.

My own bed.

Being told to turn off the light.

The sense of belonging

Ethan.

She paused at that last word. Then underlined it. Twice.

CHAPTER 10

It happened like most things did with Janet: out of the blue and with absolute certainty.

They were lying on the floor watching a movie. Ethan's fingers brushed Janet's as they reached for the popcorn, and neither of them pulled away this time.

"I have an idea," Janet said suddenly.

Ethan turned his head to look at her, already smiling. "Why do I feel like that sentence always changes my life?"

"Because it usually does," she replied. Then, quieter, "What if we… dated?"

Ethan blinked.

"I mean, we're kind of already doing it," Janet continued, sitting up. "We live together. We share a bathroom. You've seen me cry over math. That's basically marriage."

Ethan laughed. Janet was terrible at math.

"You're serious?" he asked.

She nodded. "Totally. It feels like the most normal thing in the world. We are safe with each other, and we are not invisible. I hate thinking this could eventually end."

He sat up too. The air between them felt charged.

"I feel the same. I can't imagine you not being here," Ethan said. "But I think we should talk to my mom. I mean, she lives here too."

Janet smiled. "Agreed. If we're doing this, we're doing it the honest way."

That evening over dinner, they told her.

Ethan's mom didn't blink. She set down her fork, looked from one to the other, then gave a small smile.

"Well," she said, "you're both thoughtful, kind, and entirely ridiculous about pretending you aren't already in love with each other."

Janet blushed furiously. Ethan turned red too.

She continued, "You're both under my roof, and I trust you. So yes, it makes sense. Just remember, once you start dating, there are real consequences if, God forbid, you fall out of love."

Janet grinned. "Not a chance."

From that night on, there were quiet changes.

They held hands during movie nights. Shared whispered jokes during dinner. Sometimes Ethan would come up behind her while she was doing dishes and wrap his arms around her waist, just to be close.

But they still focused on finishing school.

Ethan completed his courses first and spent the next few weeks helping Janet power through hers, quizzing her, typing out flashcards, and staying up with her when she struggled to focus.

"You've got this," he told her. "You're stronger than you think."

"How could I forget?" she said. "You always remind me."

Janet finished her final assignment on Wednesday.

That weekend, Ethan asked her to go for a walk. Just the two of them, down by the pond where they had fed ducks months ago. The air was warm, the trees swayed gently.

He stopped near the bench where they used to sit and talk.

"I want to show you something," he said, turning to her.

Janet raised an eyebrow. "Did I forget something?"

"Come on." Ethan took Janet's hand and guided her to a large tree by the water.

He pointed to the trunk. There was *E. P. + J. R.* carved into the bark, inside a heart. Janet traced her finger over the letters, then looked at Ethan, who was down on one knee.

He pulled a small, simple ring from his jacket pocket. A silver band with a tiny emerald in the center. Modest. Beautiful.

Janet froze. "Ethan…"

"We've built something together, piece by piece. You turned my house into a home. I don't want to imagine any of it without you."

Her hands covered her mouth.

"I know we're young, and this might sound crazy, but will you marry me someday? Not today. Not tomorrow. But when the time is right… will you be my forever?"

Janet knelt down with him, tears in her eyes.

"Yes," she whispered. "Yes, absolutely yes."

They sat there in the grass, the ring on her finger catching the sun.

No rush. Just holding the moment.

CHAPTER 11

They were in line at the County Clerk's Office, Ethan fiddling with his car keys, Janet chewing on a pen cap she'd taken from the front counter. It started because they didn't know how to get married. They came down to the clerk's office to ask and learn. The clerk stood across from them with tired eyes and a strict tone.

"How old are you?" the woman asked Janet, her gaze flicking between their IDs.

"Seventeen," Janet answered plainly.

"You need a notarized parental consent form or a judge's approval to apply," the woman said, pulling out a laminated flowchart. "It's state law. Do you have a legal guardian available?"

Janet hesitated. "Not really. My mom... isn't around."

The woman stopped looking at the chart. Her eyes rose slowly. "You're living alone?"

Ethan stepped in. "She's been staying with my family."

The clerk's look hardened. "I'll need to notify family services. If you're an unaccompanied minor, that's reportable."

They left the office quietly. Neither of them spoke on the way to the car.

Two days later, a knock came at Ethan's front door. A woman with a laminated badge reading *Child Protective Services* stood politely, clipboard in hand.

"Janet Rhodes?" she asked, though she already knew. "We received a referral from the county clerk's office. May I come in?"

Ethan's mom invited her inside with a nervous glance. Janet stood stiffly in the kitchen.

The caseworker walked through the home, making notes. She asked about sleeping arrangements, meals, school, and discipline. She was friendly enough, but her questions had barbed edges.

"Has Janet had consistent housing since her mother left?"

"I do now," Janet said.

The caseworker asked, "What about before? Does your mother know where you are?"

"No," Janet admitted.

"Do you have any extended family in the state?" the caseworker probed.

"No." Janet's face flushed as she furrowed her brow.

The worker's expression softened. "I understand this isn't ideal, but we have to look into it. I'll be contacting law enforcement for a safety interview. Also, I'll be making efforts to locate your mother."

The next step came from the local police. They arrived not with sirens, but with procedure.

A uniformed officer and a plainclothes detective came to the house the following afternoon. Ethan answered the door. The detective asked if he and Janet could speak privately.

"I'm under arrest," she said flatly.

"No," the detective replied, "but you're underage, and the living arrangement raised some questions."

They sat across from each other at the kitchen table. Ethan waited in the hallway, his fists clenched.

The detective's questions came slow and neutral. "Is Ethan pressuring you into anything?"

"No." Her eyes rolled at the suggestion.

"Has there been any physical contact that concerns you?"

Janet scoffed. "He literally threw himself over me during a fight so I wouldn't get stomped. That's the most physical contact we've had."

"Why not call CPS when your mom left?"

"I didn't want to get taken. I'm not helpless."

The detective nodded. "Still, you're seventeen. He's eighteen. You see how that looks, right?"

Janet's voice quieted. "I guess."

The next week was a blur of caseworkers, phone calls, and attempts to locate her mother. CPS sent formal requests to her mother's last known employer, pulled DMV records, and even tried her emergency contact numbers from school enrollment files.

No luck.

Every day Janet felt more like a file than a person. Then came a random encounter.

Ethan and Janet were back at City Hall, following up on paperwork that had been requested for Janet's continued enrollment in independent study. Ethan was at the counter, speaking with a receptionist who clearly didn't want to be there. Janet slouched in the chair by the wall, chewing her thumb, zoning out.

"I overheard some of your conversation," a man's voice said beside her.

She looked up, startled. A tall, middle-aged man in a gray sport coat stood nearby, briefcase in hand.

"I'm not a creep," he added quickly. "I'm a lawyer. Darren Knox."

"Okay...?" Janet looked up at him, expecting the worst.

He lowered his voice. "If CPS is involved, and the police have questions because your boyfriend is legal and you're not, you should consider emancipation."

Janet blinked. "That's... a real thing?"

"Yes," Knox said. "If you can show you're living independently, attending school, and financially stable — or supported in a safe way — it's possible. You'd become your own legal guardian. You could sign contracts, choose where to live, make your own education and medical decisions."

"What about CPS?"

He nodded. "They would have to close the case. No more visits. No risk of getting pulled into foster care or sent back to a parent who abandoned you."

Ethan joined them, holding a folder in one hand. "What's the catch?"

"No catch. Just red tape. You'll need to file with the juvenile court. There's a hearing. A judge will want to see documentation — living situation, income, academic records, character letters. I've got the forms in my office."

He reached into his briefcase and pulled out a thin packet.

"I'm not billing you. If you want help, take this. Fill it out. Call me if you get stuck. You've got a solid case, especially with what you've been through."

He handed them the forms and a crisp white card.

Darren Knox, J.D.

Family & Juvenile Law

(232) 515-2134

In the Camaro, the packet sat on Janet's lap like a passport.

"Think it'll work?" Ethan asked, keeping his eyes on the road.

"I don't know," she said honestly. "But for the first time in my life, it feels like maybe I can make my own rules."

He smiled, not quite at her, but with her. "Sounds like a Janet kind of idea."

She grinned. "Better believe it."

The courtroom was smaller than Janet expected. No echoing marble floors, no jury box — just a square room with paneled walls, a judge's bench raised modestly at the far end, and a few rows of wooden benches behind a rail.

Ethan sat in the front row, hands clenched between his knees, his shirt still slightly wrinkled from helping Janet reprint documents that morning. He gave her a nod. She gave him a small, twitchy smirk in return — her version of brave.

At the front of the room, Janet stood alone beside a modest podium. A bailiff called her case number. The judge, Honorable Wallace Granger, adjusted his glasses and peered at the stack of papers in front of him.

"Janet Rhodes," he said, voice low and neutral. "You're petitioning for emancipation under M.E.R. 12-2451?"

"Yes, Your Honor," Janet answered in a shaky voice.

"You've submitted documentation of your residence, school enrollment, and support letters from two adults. One being a former school teacher, the other... Ethan Parker, listed here as a friend and temporary guardian."

"Yes, sir," Janet replied.

The judge nodded and flipped through the file slowly. Janet stood perfectly still. The silence in the room buzzed louder than any crowd ever had.

"Before I make a decision," the judge said, "I need to understand who you are. Why do you want this?"

Janet took a deep breath. "Because I want control over my life. Because I've been making adult decisions for a long time, without anyone asking if I was ready. Because my mom left, and I've been taking care of myself ever since. Because no one else was going to do it for me."

Granger tilted his head. "What about the risks? What if you fail?"

"I've already failed," she said plainly. "And I got back up. I think that means I'm ready to keep trying, legally or not."

He tapped his pen on the bench. "You live with Mr. Parker's family?"

"Yes. They treat me as family."

"He's eighteen?"

"Yes."

"Has he ever exerted control over you — financially, emotionally, romantically?"

Janet shook her head. "No. Ethan is... he's kind. Protective. Gallant, even. He treats me like I matter, but never like I belong to him."

Granger raised an eyebrow. "Gallant? That's an unusual word for a teenager to use."

Janet's mouth twitched. "He reads to me."

The judge chuckled softly and turned the page. "You've remained in school. Your grades have improved since transferring to independent study. You submitted grocery receipts, bus passes, even a phone bill in your name. You've done your homework."

"Yes, sir," Janet affirmed.

Another long pause. Judge Granger stacked the papers together and leaned back in his chair. The room went completely still. Ethan stopped breathing.

The judge narrowed his eyes with theatrical flair and said, "Well. This is highly irregular. Borderline controversial."

Janet's heart thundered.

"But..." he continued, straightening the folder and giving her a rare, slight smile, "sometimes, irregular people are the ones who survive — even thrive."

He tapped his gavel lightly once on the bench.

"Ms. Janet Rhodes, as of this day, you are hereby recognized as a legal adult under the laws of this state. Your emancipation is granted."

Janet blinked. "Wait, really?"

Granger smiled more fully now. "With all due respect, I think I just said that on the record."

Behind her, Ethan finally exhaled. Janet turned just in time to see him lean back, hand over his chest in dramatic relief.

The judge raised an eyebrow. "Now, about this Mr. Parker. If he sticks around, and if there's ever a wedding..."

Janet laughed, almost breathless. "You want an invitation?"

"I'd expect nothing less," Granger said. "I don't attend many fairy tales. It's nice to see one with documentation."

Outside the courthouse, the wind was sharp and alive. Janet stepped down the stone steps slowly, feeling her feet touch the ground like it was somehow hers now.

Ethan was already waiting near the Camaro, holding out his hand like a butler greeting royalty.

"Miss Rhodes," he said with a playful bow, "you're a free woman."

Janet didn't take his hand.

She crashed into his chest and held him tight.

CHAPTER 12

The kitchen was quiet, except for the clink of spoons scraping cereal bowls and the low hum of the fridge. Outside, the late morning sun filtered through the blinds in slanted stripes across the tile. Ethan and Janet sat at the small table, still in pajama pants, bare feet tucked beneath their chairs, with the last of Ethan's mom's coffee between them.

It was one of those rare calm moments. No paperwork. No court dates. No school officials. No bruises fading on their faces. Just quiet.

Janet set her spoon down and leaned back in her chair.

"I have an idea."

Ethan looked up slowly, his mouth already curling into a cautious smile. "Of course you do."

"No, seriously," she said, brushing her hair out of her face. "What are we even waiting for?"

He blinked. "Waiting for what?"

She looked him dead in the eye. "Let's just get married."

Ethan froze.

Janet kept going. "I mean, think about it. There are no more hoops to jump through. I'm emancipated. You're legal. We already had our background check courtesy of the state, and we've got a stack of signed affidavits saying we're not criminals."

Ethan set his hot chocolate down more slowly than he meant to. "That's not how people usually decide to get married."

Janet tilted her head. "Why not? We're planning to anyway. What's going to be different six months from now? Or in a year? Or two? We're not doing this for the flowers or the fancy photos. We're already us."

He studied her face. There was no smirk, no teasing glint. She wasn't messing with him. She was serious, and maybe a little scared.

"You don't think it's too fast?" he asked gently.

"I think everything else in my life has been too slow. Too uncertain. Too temporary. You're the only thing that's felt... solid. And we've already been through the worst parts. Everything after this? That's the easy part."

Ethan exhaled and leaned back in his chair, rubbing the bridge of his nose.

"I mean… I always thought if I got married, it would be years from now. After college. After I figured out what I'm doing."

Janet shrugged. "You are doing something. You're showing up. You're helping me build a life. You're the one thing that doesn't disappear on me."

They sat in silence for a long time. Not uncomfortable. Just... full.

Finally, Ethan reached across the table and took her hand.

"So this is the next Janet idea?"

She nodded, the faintest grin tugging at her lips. "The biggest one yet."

He looked at their intertwined fingers. And for the first time, the idea didn't terrify him.

It just felt right.

Ethan's mom was drying dishes when they told her.

Janet stood at the edge of the kitchen, arms folded like a shield, but her voice was steady. "We want to get married."

Ethan sat beside her, calm but ready to step in if needed. His mother turned slowly, dish towel still in her hand, the plate halfway to the cabinet.

She blinked once, then twice.

"I… okay," she said cautiously. "That's not exactly how I expected my Wednesday to go."

Janet jumped in before the objections could form. "Nothing changes. We'll still live here. We'll both get jobs.

We already talked about it. Rent, groceries, bills, chores. Everything."

"It'll just be more official," Ethan added. "And honestly, we're already acting like a family."

Janet glanced toward the living room and the small back office that had doubled as her bedroom these past few weeks. "Plus, you get your office back."

That earned a raised eyebrow and the faintest smirk from Ethan's mom. She leaned back against the counter, crossing her arms and studying them both with that specific mystical mother x-ray vision.

"Are you doing this because of love," she asked softly, "or because you're afraid the world's going to take you away from each other?"

Janet and Ethan answered together. "Both."

The pause was long, but not heavy.

Finally, Ethan's mom sighed, and a small smile tugged at the corner of her mouth. "Alright, let's do it right."

They made the call that afternoon. The Justice of the Peace had an opening on Friday, late morning. A quiet courthouse ceremony. Nothing big. No fanfare. Just two kids who had already seen enough of life to know what they wanted. Word got around faster than either of them expected.

The judge who had granted Janet's emancipation showed up in his off-hours, grinning like a proud uncle. Even Darren Knox, the lawyer who had stepped in like a plot twist in the city hall lobby, took time off to attend. He brought a card that read: *The best contracts are made with trust.*

And then there was Janet. Ethan's mom had pulled out her old wedding dress. Ivory satin, delicate embroidery, a little off-white now, but still beautiful. Janet held it up and whispered, "Are you sure?"

"Yes, of course. I'm thrilled Ethan's bride would want to wear my dress," Ethan's mom said.

It was a little loose around the waist and a bit too long. They pinned it and folded the fabric with safety pins and patience. And when Janet stepped out of the bathroom that morning, she looked like a dream people only hope for.

Ethan stood at the front in a button-up shirt and his best slacks, his tie slightly crooked, his hands nervously fiddling with the cuffs. But when he saw her, he froze, like time had pressed pause just for them.

She didn't need a bouquet. She didn't need music.

She just needed Ethan, waiting for her like he always did, with steady eyes and room to breathe.

The vows were simple. The rings were modest. The kiss was romantic, sincere, and impossibly tender.

And when the Justice of the Peace smiled and said, "You are husband and wife," Janet whispered, almost giddy, "I have an idea…"

Ethan's laugh escaped before he could catch it, forehead against hers. "I knew you would."

Time didn't fly. It settled in comfortably.

The Camaro still rumbled to life every morning at 6:45, and Ethan and Janet still had breakfast together at the small kitchen table. Sometimes it was cereal, other times pancakes or eggs, usually depending on who woke up first. No matter what, they always sat down at the same time, side by side, brushing shoulders, laughing about work stories or arguing about whose turn it was to take out the trash.

It was the sweetest kind of ordinary.

They had both picked up jobs after their wedding. Ethan worked full-time shifts with his uncle's construction crew. There was talk of giving him his own team as the company grew. Janet took a part-time receptionist job at the law firm where Darren Knox worked. She liked talking with families during those stressful times. It gave her a sense of worth, helping to comfort people as they worked through the system.

But one morning, everything paused.

Janet didn't eat her toast. She sat with her fingers wrapped around a mug she hadn't sipped from yet, watching the steam curl into the air. Ethan's mom—now officially *Mom* to Janet—was flipping through a grocery ad at the counter.

Ethan looked over, fork halfway to his mouth. "You okay?"

Janet gave a quiet little smile and turned to Mom.

"Hey," she said gently. "Remember how we said nothing would change when we got married?"

Mom looked up.

Janet exhaled and glanced down, placing a hand against her lower belly. It wasn't obvious yet—not to most people—but to her, it felt like carrying a secret that had started to glow.

"Well, something has changed."

Ethan's fork dropped to the plate with a soft clink.

Mom blinked, her face blank for just a heartbeat.

Then Janet added, voice calm but sure, "We're going to have a baby."

Ethan's mother let out a breath that turned into the softest kind of laugh—the stunned, joyful kind people make when something sacred sneaks up on them.

"You're... oh my, I get to be a grandma." Mom teared up.

Janet nodded, sheepish but glowing.

Ethan finally found his voice. "How do you know?"

"I took a test. Actually, I took three of them," Janet admitted. "I wanted to be sure before I said anything."

Mom stood, hand over her mouth for a moment, then crossed the room and pulled Janet into her arms. "You are going to be such a good mom," she whispered.

Janet clung to her, caught off guard by how much that meant—how much she needed to hear it.

Then, true to form, Ethan's mom shifted gears. She pulled a notepad from the drawer and tapped a pen against it like a general before a battle.

"We need a list. Diapers. A crib. Clothes. Bottles."

"There's time," Janet reassured them both. "We're okay."

She looked at Ethan, and he took her hand without hesitation. For the first time in his life, he didn't feel like a kid pretending to be the man of the house. He just felt like a husband—and soon, a dad.

The morning sunlight streamed through the windows in golden streaks, warming the baby onesies Janet had laid out on the table. There were three of them: soft cotton, tiny snaps, and prints so small and delicate it made her heart feel like it might burst.

"This one," Janet said, holding up a yellow sleeper with a duck on the front, "is for when we bring the baby home from the hospital."

Ethan, still lacing his work boots, looked up and grinned. "That's a power move. You're already picking outfits like a pro."

Janet laughed and pressed the tiny onesie to her chest, swaying like she was already holding the baby. "I just want them to feel loved right away, you know?"

Ethan stood and crossed the kitchen, wrapping his arms around her from behind and resting his chin on her shoulder. "They will. You're gonna love the heck out of this kid."

Janet leaned back against him, closing her eyes. "I'm getting excited now. I was nervous at first. It felt like I'd lose this if I got too attached."

They kissed, soft and sure. Then Ethan grabbed his lunch and headed out the door, tossing a wink over his shoulder.

Janet watched him go, heart full. She didn't expect the pain to come so suddenly.

It was like the floor moved under her. One moment she was loading the dishwasher beside Mom, the next, her knees buckled and the room spun.

She clutched the edge of the counter, her breath shallow. "Something's wrong."

Then everything went white.

Mom's hands were shaking as she helped the nurse fill out the intake paperwork at the hospital. Janet seemed alert but was pale and disoriented, her words slurring just slightly. They'd rushed her back for tests—bloodwork, fetal monitoring, fluids, heart rate checks.

She was stable, but no one had answers yet. That was when Ethan burst through the ER doors.

His boots echoed on the tile as he ran to the front desk, eyes wild. "Janet Parker. My wife. She was brought in."

A nurse recognized his urgent tone. "She's stable, sir. Room 312. Just one visitor at a time." She handed him a visitor sticker.

Ethan didn't wait. He sprinted down the hall.

When he reached the room and saw her—propped up in the hospital bed with an IV taped to her arm and leads on her belly—he stopped like someone had cut the air from his lungs.

"Hey," Janet said weakly. "I'm okay."

Ethan didn't speak, not at first. He crossed to her, sat carefully on the edge of the bed, and took her hand. His eyes were wet, his lips quivering. His thumb kept brushing over hers, like he needed to keep touching her to make sure she was real.

"I was so scared. It felt just like when we got the call about Dad," he whispered hoarsely.

"They're testing now, but I feel okay," Janet reassured him.

"I thought... I thought I was going to lose you. I couldn't breathe."

Her face softened, tears welling up. "I was scared too."

"Our baby is okay?" Ethan leaned forward, resting his forehead against the back of her hand.

Janet pointed to a quiet monitor beside them. It beeped steadily, marking the tiny heartbeat that had become the center of their world.

"I am so glad you're both okay." He held her hand firmly, his touch saying everything his words couldn't.

CHAPTER 13

The hospital room had gone quiet. The steady beeping of the fetal monitor was the only sound filling the space—gentle and rhythmic, a heartbeat within a heartbeat.

Dr. Kaul, a soft-spoken neurologist with kind eyes and a clipboard full of gravity, had just checked on Janet. He hadn't confirmed anything. Not officially. But he had said the word. Glioblastoma.

He thought it could explain the lightheadedness, her collapse, and the headaches. Janet hadn't paid much attention to her symptoms. She thought they were related to pregnancy. They were doing scans, more tests. They'd know more soon.

That word had landed in the room like a brick through glass.

Janet sat still, staring at the far wall. Her hand rested over her belly, protective and instinctual. Ethan sat beside her, elbows on his knees, eyes fixed on her. Afraid if he lost sight of her, she would disappear.

For the longest time, neither spoke.

Finally, Janet broke the silence. Her voice was small, like she was scared to hear herself say it. "He said brain tumor."

Ethan's jaw clenched. "He said they don't know for sure. Not yet."

"Yeah." She nodded, and a single tear rolled down her cheek. "But we both heard what he thinks."

Ethan looked at her then. Really looked. Her strength. Her fight. Her fire. And under all of that, her fear.

Without thinking, he sat down on the edge of the hospital bed beside her so he could hold both of her hands in his. His voice cracked. "That first day in detention, I would have given anything to get away from you, but now I can't imagine my life without you."

Tears welled in her eyes, and her bottom lip trembled. "I'm not going anywhere. I didn't even know if this life was possible for me. I've never had something I wanted to hold on to like this."

Ethan pressed her hands to his lips. "Then hold on. You hear me? We are fighters, and this time I won't cover you so you can fight. Whatever comes, we can take it."

She reached out, brushing her fingers through his hair, her touch soft. "I love you, Ethan Parker. I knew it since our detention."

He smiled through the tears. "You make it easy. I'd do anything for you, Janet."

She exhaled a weak laugh and rested her forehead against his. "This baby deserves the chance to know their dad. And I'm going to do everything to make sure they know their mom, too."

He kissed her forehead.

They sat like that for a long time, on the edge of what if, wrapped in the comfort of the other being there. No matter

what came next, they had each other. That meant they still had everything.

The lights in the hospital room had been dimmed hours ago, but no one had slept.

Janet lay curled on her side, the blanket pulled to her chin, her eyes glassy and unmoving. Ethan sat close, legs drawn up in the visitor chair, hands locked tightly in his lap. He hadn't said a word since the doctor left.

"Janet," Dr. Kaul said gently, "the MRI confirms what I suspected. There is a mass in your brain stem. It's consistent with glioblastoma, and it's aggressive."

Treatment could buy them time—maybe a year—if everything went perfectly. But there was a cost. The chemotherapy and radiation would almost certainly end the pregnancy.

If they delayed treatment and waited until the baby was born, it would shorten Janet's life drastically. Months. Maybe less. The tumor would grow, unchecked.

The door clicked softly as the doctor pulled it shut behind her, leaving the two of them alone.

They sat there, still. No words.

Finally, Ethan spoke, his voice barely more than a whisper. "Of course it had to be cancer."

Janet's eyes fluttered closed, still processing what she had heard.

"I can't do this." He paused, then tried again. "There's no version of this that doesn't destroy me."

"I know," she murmured as a tear rolled down her face.

Another silence passed. Then she reached for his hand and pulled it to rest over her belly. Their baby kicked softly beneath his palm.

"That's ours," she said. "That's a whole life. You and I are in this baby."

Ethan swallowed hard, staring at her. "I can't. I don't know what to do. Tell me what to do."

"My life is ending," she said gently. "I don't know when, but it's coming."

Tears welled in his eyes, and she pulled his hand to her chest.

"We've talked about everything, Ethan. Every plan, every dream, every dumb idea."

She looked at him, her lips trembling. "I have one more idea."

He gave a sputtering laugh through tears. "Of course you do."

She took a breath, deep and shaking. "We must give this baby a chance. A real one. Even if it costs us everything."

Ethan's face crumpled, and she cupped his cheek, steadying him as the tears fell.

"I want to live, Ethan. I'm not giving up, but I can't take life from our baby to have maybe a few more months. That's not the mom I want to be."

His forehead rested against hers, both of them broken open and raw.

"Tell me what to do," he whispered. "I will do whatever you ask me to do."

Janet held him. "I want you to tell our baby stories. Every single one. I want them to know who I was. I didn't run off like my mom did."

"I will," he said, tears slipping down his cheeks and landing in her hair.

They stayed like that for a long time, no longer searching for answers, only holding each other like the world had narrowed to a heartbeat and a decision.

Outside the window, the first light of morning began to glow, painting the hospital walls in gold. They no longer had a choice to make. There was only one idea left, and it was everything.

Janet was fighting so their child would live.

CHAPTER 14

Janet had gone into labor just after midnight. No warning, no time to prepare. It was two weeks early, but close enough that her baby had the best chance Janet could give her. She'd poked at Ethan and said, "It's happening."

The doctors were already on alert. The high-risk team moved quickly, voices calm but urgent, ushering Janet into delivery with precision and care. She was so pale. So thin. Her strength was fading, but her stubborn will was ready to do whatever she had to.

"I want to see her," she said with conviction between contractions. "I want to hold her. I have to."

"You will," Ethan said, gripping her hand with everything he had. "You will."

At 3:26 a.m., their daughter entered the world with a fierce cry, the sound high and healthy. Ethan swore time stopped. He felt a warmth pass through him. The nurses wrapped her in a soft white blanket and gently placed her in his arms.

He stared at her, overwhelmed. She was perfect. Tiny fists, blinking eyes, dark wisps of hair. The most beautiful girl in the world. He shifted as he held her, moving to bring her to Janet.

Janet was exhausted, her body wrecked from the strain, but when Ethan sat beside her and placed the baby in her arms, she rallied. Her arms trembled, but she held on tight.

"Hi, sweetheart," she whispered, brushing her lips across the baby's forehead. "I'm your mama."

Tears fell freely down her cheeks, but her voice was steady. "You are worth it. I'd give you everything."

Ethan sat beside them, one arm around Janet, one hand supporting the baby. Their little family. In this moment, it was everything they'd dreamed of.

The baby drifted off in her arms, and Janet smiled.

"I'm tired too," she said, turning to Ethan. "Will you sit with us for a while?"

He nodded, gently holding the baby in her arms.

He sat there holding his little family together. Their daughter, in the soft light of morning, looked like an angel. Janet's breathing slowed, her chest rising and falling like a lullaby, until it stopped.

In his arms, their daughter stirred. A soft sigh escaped her lips, and a tiny fist curled against his chest. He looked down at the bundle cradled in his arms and remembered what Janet had asked him to do. He kissed her forehead; the same spot Janet had kissed just hours before.

Ethan had just walked through the door from work when a little girl with curly dark hair and small combat boots came around the corner.

"Dad, I have an idea," she said with confidence.

Ethan's eyes filled with tears. "What is it, baby girl?"

She simply said, "Will you take me to talk to Mommy?"

The gravestone was simple, just the way Janet would have wanted:

JANET PARKER

Wife. Mother. Friend.

"I have an idea."

Ethan traced the words with his eyes, as if reading them for the hundredth time might somehow bring her voice back to him.

He laid out a blanket, and they sat together in the peaceful breeze. Ethan listened as his little girl told her mom about all the adventures, they'd had that week.

He looked at his father's headstone beside Janet's. "Look after her for me."

Then he heard his daughter ask, "What were the ducks' names? I forgot again."

After she finished talking to her mom, she turned to Ethan.

"Will you tell me about her?"

"Her name was Janet. And she was... trouble," he said with a chuckle. "The beautiful, brilliant kind. She never knocked before entering a room or a life. She just walked in like she belonged, because she did."

"She was loud, and smart, and annoying in all the best ways. She made fun of my car the first time she saw it, then defended it like it was sacred when someone else tried."

"Yeah. She was like that. Rough edges with a soft heart. She teased me and gave me a hard time, but I couldn't stand it when she wasn't around."

His voice caught in his throat. He swallowed and steadied himself. His daughter nestled into his chest, happy to stay there. Ethan held her gently.

"You know you are just like her."

"Is that why we have the same name?" she asked.

"Yes, little Janet," Ethan admitted.

"I miss her all the time, but you remind me of her, so it's not as bad."

Little Janet climbed onto Ethan's back. He hiked her up and held her securely.

"I have an idea," she said. "Can we get ice cream on the way home?"

"Ice cream does fix everything."